SPECIAL MESSAGE TO READERS

THE ULVERSCROFT FOUNDATION
(registered UK charity number 264873)
was established in 1972 to provide funds for
research, diagnosis and treatment of eye diseases.
Examples of major projects funded by
the Ulverscroft Foundation are:-

- The Children's Eye Unit at Moorfields Eye Hospital, London
- The Ulverscroft Children's Eye Unit at Great Ormond Street Hospital for Sick Children
- Funding research into eye diseases and treatment at the Department of Ophthalmology, University of Leicester
- The Ulverscroft Vision Research Group, Institute of Child Health
- Twin operating theatres at the Western Ophthalmic Hospital, London
- The Chair of Ophthalmology at the Royal Australian College of Ophthalmologists

You can help further the work of the Foundation
by making a donation or leaving a legacy.
Every contribution is gratefully received. If you
would like to help support the Foundation or
require further information, please contact:

THE ULVERSCROFT FOUNDATION
The Green, Bradgate Road, Anstey
Leicester LE7 7FU, England
Tel: (0116) 236 4325
website: www.foundation.ulverscroft.com

FURY DRIVES BY NIGHT

Captain Guy Conway of the British Secret Intelligence sets out to investigate Fortune Cay, a three-hundred-year-old cottage on the Yorkshire coast. The current owner is being terrorised by his new neighbour, who Guy fears could be his arch-nemesis, an international mercenary and war criminal whom he thought he had killed towards the end of the Second World War. En route to the cottage, Conway rescues an unconscious woman from her crashed car — only to find that their lives are inextricably linked as they fight to cheat death . . .

Books by Denis Hughes
in the Linford Mystery Library:

DEATH WARRIORS

DENIS HUGHES

FURY DRIVES
BY NIGHT

Complete and Unabridged

LINFORD
Leicester

First published in Great Britain

First Linford Edition
published 2017

A catalogue record for this book is available
from the British Library.

ISBN 978–1–4448–3240–2

1

With tyres crunching gently on the wide sweep of gravelled drive, the big car pulled up at the door of Verity Hall. It was a long-bonneted machine; powerful, almost ugly, certainly outrageous in most respects; in the illegal noise of its exhaust, for instance, its entire absence of weather protection, the fast lines of its rakish, dusty body.

When Captain Guy Conway pushed up his goggles, slid out from behind the wheel and, ignoring the apology for a door, swung long legs over the side to the ground, a casual observer might have noticed a marked similarity of character between the car and its driver. Clad in baggy corduroys and a sports shirt open at the neck, he gave the same impression of untidy carelessness as the car behind him. But then, of course, unlike the man who watched him from the library window, a casual observer would not have known him for what he was — one of the most valuable agents British Secret

Intelligence numbered on its payroll.

Behind the indolent exterior lay an amazingly active brain, and, in the spring of his step and the lithe strength of his lean, hard body, was hidden something akin to the speed and agility of a tiger.

'Deceptive as the devil himself,' was how Sir Randolph Guildford had once described his visitor, and with a smile of pleasure on his leathery features, he unlatched the tall French windows and stepped out to the sun-drenched terrace beyond.

'Come in this way, Guy,' he called heartily and, moving aside as the younger man came up, led him through to the cool library. 'Sit down. Make yourself comfortable. Drink?'

'Thanks, I'd love one, sir — Scotch with plenty of soda if you can manage it.' He looked round, his lazy grey eyes taking in every detail of the room; a room he knew well, a room in which many perilous adventures had found their beginning and many tales been told.

His host, Sir Randolph Guildford, owner of Verity Hall and the brain behind a vast machine of intrigue of which Guy was but one small part, had already started mixing drinks. 'What's in the wind this time, sir?'

'I'm not at all sure, Guy. It's you who are going to find out, I hope.' Guy waited in silence as he went on: 'Does the name Peter Mersey convey anything to you?'

'He's an artist of some sort, isn't he?'

Sir Randolph inclined his head. 'Black and white, and watercolour seascapes,' he enlarged in a satisfied tone.

More pieces fell into place in Guy's mind. 'That's it — I remember now, sir. I read a news item about him some time ago. Lives on the coast somewhere up north; bought a cottage there shortly after the war ended. He was wounded pretty badly at Caen if I'm not mistaken.'

Sir Randolph rose from his chair and walked over to the big desk occupying one whole corner of the room. Shifting some papers aside, he picked up an envelope. 'Help yourself to another drink while I tell you what I can,' he said.

Guy manipulated decanter and syphon with expert skill, and before his glass was half full the other man began: 'I know Mersey fairly well. He used to be a quiet, easy-going

3

young man six months back. Self-contained, I'd call him. When he came down here about three weeks ago to see my niece, I was shocked at the change in the fellow.'

'How do you mean, sir?' put in Guy.

'Jittery, nervy, and obviously deeply worried about something. I tried a little careful pumping but got no change out of it — he's an independent sort of chap, more likely to nurse trouble than share it with anyone, if you know what I mean.'

Guy nodded.

'Which made it all the more surprising when I received letter from him on Monday.' He held out the envelope and Guy took it, removing from inside a page of closely spaced writing.

Before he could start reading it, however, Sir Randolph went on: 'Mersey lives in Yorkshire. His cottage stands right on the coast at the top of a cliff, and delights in the name Fortune Cay. It's a lonely little stone-built place at least three hundred years old. Local gossip has it that a retired pirate built it and named it after his Caribbean Sea base.

'At the foot of the cliff is a very small

inlet, just about large enough to harbour a motor boat, and there Mersey keeps his sailing dinghy. A path, or a series of steps, I should say, cut in the cliff face itself gives access to the shore from above, while on the landward side the place is reached by a rough track over the moor from the main road.' He paused. 'I think that's about all I can tell you. Now go ahead and read his extraordinary letter. I'll be interested to know what you make of it.'

Hoisting himself up in his chair, Guy complied.

Fortune Cay,
Yorkshire, 10th August, 1947

Dear Sir Randolph,
I think that on my last visit to Verity Hall you realised I was not quite myself. The fact of the matter is that I should appreciate your advice more than I can say.

If my suspicions have any foundations, something very strange is going on in this isolated corner of England, including a plot to drive me out of Fortune Cay; not by outright methods which I could combat effectively, but by subtle and diabolical cunning. The trouble is, I have not one shred of real proof or evidence to support my doubts.

As you may remember, there is an enormous half-derelict house called Pardoner's Folly standing about a mile inland from Fortune Cay. After being empty for years it is now occupied. Five weeks ago a man named Richmond bought it and moved in. As far as I can make out from current gossip, he lives in one or two rooms only, has no dealings with the village six miles away, and is maintained in solitary state by two manservants who bear a close resemblance to gorillas, one of whom I hear is a deaf-mute. Richmond himself is a peculiar person. An evil-looking, one-eyed fellow who walks with a limp, yet is well-spoken and obviously a cultured man.

Our first contact was unpleasant. From the cottage to the village there is a short cut over the moors by a path running across one corner of the land round Pardoner's Folly. Somewhat naturally I have been in the habit of using it, and saw no reason why I should discontinue. Richmond, however, resented my action. One morning he barred my way and told me in no uncertain terms that I was trespassing; in fact, he ordered me off. Admittedly the short cut is not a public path, and the man was within his rights, but his manner was aggressive out of all proportion to the crime.

Regan, my Alsatian, almost flew at his throat, and I think that in spite of his threats and bluster the fellow was scared stiff. A couple of days later the dog went out and never returned. Naturally I searched next day and found his body at the foot of the cliff. He could have fallen over, I suppose, but he was an exceptionally sure-footed animal, and I had my doubts.

And now there is the water. Isolated as this place is, I depend on a well which is open and unprotected. A week ago I found it contained the rotting carcass of a sheep and is now, of course, polluted. To the best of my knowledge no sheep have been near here during all the time I have lived here, and I am certain it was no accident, just as I feel sure Richmond wants me out of the way for some reason. Something is going on behind the scenes, and frankly the whole business is getting on my nerves. Only obstinacy keeps me here, but even that is wearing thin; yet on the other hand I hate the idea of giving up.

I have one possible notion to account for all this, but in the cold light of day it sounds so fantastic that I would rather not mention it until I hear from you or see you personally.

I hope you will not think this letter too much of an impertinence.

Yours, etc., etc.

Guy folded the sheet thoughtfully and looked at Sir Randolph. 'I have a feeling that I'm going to dislike this merchant Richmond intensely, sir.' He spoke quietly, and his eyes were no longer lazy. The rather satanic lines of his face hardened as he went on: 'This is all we have to work on, is it?'

Sir Randolph took the letter and tapped it on the ends of his fingers. 'Doesn't Richmond strike you as familiar?'

Guy frowned. 'Richmond?' Suddenly he shot upright, an unholy ghost of suspicion boring its way into his brain. It couldn't be! Striding to the window, he gazed out on the glory of sun-splashed parkland. This was England; here was Reason and Sanity, but the other ... He spun round to meet the unsmiling stare of the older man. 'You're thinking the same as I am, sir?' The question was almost defiant, but Sir Randolph merely nodded and uttered two words: 'Craig Tyler.'

Guy fought against it unbelievingly. The name spelt intrigue, peril, and sudden death. Richmond and Tyler simply could not be one and the same. Craig Tyler was dead; thrown to his fate by Guy's own hands from a railway viaduct in Italy four years previously. He had to be dead. Yet this man Richmond — clever, cultured, blind in one eye and with an undisguisable limp ... The description fitted perfectly, as did Mersey's impression of his character. Then there was his fear of the dog. Probably the only thing Tyler had been afraid of was a dog. Odd but true. It all fitted in an uncanny way, but still Guy blinked at the possibility. How could Tyler, international criminal, cosmopolitan soldier of fortune, a man who would sell his services and his brain to the highest bidder, be here in England, alive? Guy refused to credit the fact as proven, but was forced to admit that Tyler could have escaped death. Only too well did he know how far the long arm of coincidence could reach. The man's fall might have been broken by trees or water, for instance. Thinking back, it had been a pitch dark night, and Guy had not been able to see the result of his act.

Accepting the possibility meant admitting a previous failure, but it also meant the birth of a second opportunity to even the score. Guy stubbed out his cigarette and lit another, then moved from the window to the fireplace. His hands were thrust deep in his pockets and the old smile crept back to his lips, sensing the cigarette raking upwards at an acute angle. 'Have you any inkling of what he's up to, sir?'

'No, I'm afraid not, but assuming that Richmond is Tyler, it's sure to be something pretty devilish, and it's clear that for some reason or other he is very anxious to get

Mersey out of Fortune Cay. Can you think of any sound reason why a man of our friend's calibre should want to establish himself on a rocky, isolated stretch of coast in Yorkshire?'

Guy inhaled a lungful of smoke and squinted up at the oak-beamed ceiling. 'I think I'd plump for smuggling in some form or other. Especially in view of the little sea inlet you told me about.'

'My own notion, too, but I want to be sure. If Tyler is really back in circulation, I can't help feeling that there's something bigger in the pot than we suspect — smuggling strikes me as a little tame for our friend somehow. I want you to go and have a look round, but treat it as an unofficial case for the moment — it may develop. If it does turn out to be smuggling, the excise people can handle it.'

He walked on to the terrace and gazed with strangely unseeing eyes at the distant hills. For a full minute he remained still, then turned to face the room again. 'We can't afford to have men like him running loose in England, Guy.' His voice was deadly serious.

'No, sir, you're right there.'

Their eyes met. These two men, who knew and understood each other so well, found the moment more awkward than it should have been. Sir Randolph, protective as he was of the safety of his country, was human enough to realise that when he sent a man out he might easily be sending him to his death. He looked suddenly tired, as if feeling the strain of his position.

Guy held out his hand. 'I'll let you know the moment I have anything tangible to report, sir.' His tone was light, but his mind was tuned to the feel of coming danger.

A few seconds later Sir Randolph was watching the Bentley disappear down the drive, and for five minutes afterwards as he stood listening, there came to his ears on the still air the gradually fading howl of its exhaust and the high-pitched whine of a supercharger as the driver opened up on the Great North Road.

Captain Guy Conway, like an overtaking Nemesis, was on his way, and if Richmond could have seen the light of battle flickering in his eyes he might have thought twice before carrying on with his plans.

2

When Guy settled down to cover a large mileage, he did it as thoroughly as he did anything, and by early evening had located the moorland track which led to Peter Mersey's cottage.

Turning down it, he drove slowly until he judged that roughly half the distance lay behind him; and then, finding a suitably concealed hollow on one side, he let the big car run gently off the track to the cover of a tangled mass of undergrowth.

He never considered it good policy to advertise his presence to anyone until the right moment. A habit acquired from long experience, he found that more often than not it paid high dividends, both in the element of surprise it offered, and by the insurance of resulting caution.

Standing by the running board, he reached across and transferred a small automatic from the cubbyhole in the dash to his hip pocket, and then, with a final glance round, set off down the rutted path in the direction of the sea.

Topping a rise, he saw stretched out in front of him a wide saucer of weathered brown moor; and in the distance, where the swell of earth gave place to an intensely blue canvas of sea, stood the crouching outline of a grey stone cottage. Fortune Cay — for the grey stone cottage could be no other — seemed to balance on the jagged hairline where land met sea, teetering on the very brink of the cliffs as it gave the impression of swaying in the strange distortion of heat which rose in an invisible haze from the sweltering waste of dried-up grass and bracken between. It looked almost insecure perched there on the razor edge of cliff that dropped away sheer to the tumbling waves below. White-bellied seagulls wheeled and dived above and around its time-shaded roof, fitting perfectly into the scene.

So that was Fortune Cay, thought Guy, and he turned his attention to the further boundaries of the landscape before him. From his vantage point he could see that the shallow depression below him was almost entirely devoid of trees except for

14

one large plantation away to the left. Rising from their dark green shadow was a cluster of chimneys which he realised must belong to Pardoner's Folly. Scanning the area carefully, he could see no sign of movement either in the vicinity of the plantation or the cottage. The westering sun had almost disappeared, and only its last glow now touched the scene with flaming fingers, painting harsh lines among the bracken and gorse, or tipping the naked, frowning tors with a blood-like rouge.

The dusty track that had brought him so far continued straight from where he stood to the door of Fortune Cay itself, but was joined about fifty yards from his present position by a wider, rather more overgrown branch leading to the plantation of trees that sheltered Richmond's house.

Guy was on the point of starting off again down the slope towards the cottage when a smudge of movement at the edge of the trees caught his roving attention, and watching closely for a few seconds he saw it materialise into the beetle shape of a large American saloon. Stirring a thin cloud of dust by its passage, it sped down the track, and instinctively Guy retired to the shelter of a ragged gorse bush. Dropping out of sight, he waited for the car to pass; and as it drew level, sleek and shining in its opulent display of chromium plate, he caught a glimpse of the sole occupant. In the fleeting second before the car swept by and was gone, his eyes had registered and retained for always the features of a heavy face: red ears, long nose, pig eyes. He saw, too, the cigar, and a flash of diamonds on one white pudgy hand. Clearly a man of some substance! Guy wondered who he might be and was determined to find out at the earliest opportunity. Anyone who came and went in the proximity of Pardoner's Folly was interesting and worthy of note.

Screwing up his eyes against the dust, he just had time to read and remember the registration number of the swiftly receding vehicle, and then sat down to consider his next move. He would prefer it if Mersey knew nothing of his connection with Sir Randolph — for the moment anyway — and least of all did he want the man to think he was prying into his affairs. In view of this a casual meeting was indicated, and what more natural than for him to approach the cottage on the pretext of being lost? His clothes would bear out the lie that he was a member of some rambling club who had missed his way, and once entry was gained to the place he felt sure he could rely on his wits to prolong the visit and find a chance to probe the secret that made Richmond so anxious to uproot Mersey.

Having made up his mind, he struck off down the track, his steps muffled by the carpet of dust, his eyes keenly alert for any sign of movement. He wondered whether or not the wheeling seabirds were an ill omen. Peaceful as everything appeared to be, he distrusted the atmosphere, and though outwardly his movements remained unhurried, his brain was alive to any eventuality that might arise.

The cottage was silent and apparently deserted when he strode up to the door. Above the heavy wrought-iron knocker was pinned a piece of paper, and pulling it down he held it to the fading light.

'Dear June,' he read. 'Sorry, but I was called away unexpectedly. Make yourself at home.' The note was signed 'Peter'. Guy frowned at the words as if they offended him. The fellow would go off like that just when he was wanted, he thought. And who might 'June' be?

He felt slightly annoyed, and without thinking pushed the sheet of paper into his pocket as he moved off to circle the cottage. Peering through the windows, he could see some details of the low-ceilinged lounge that occupied most of the ground floor. In one corner a staircase mounted to the upper storey, and behind at the back, overlooking the sea, was the kitchen. All the doors and windows were firmly secured, and short of breaking in — a risky procedure before dark — he looked like drawing blank. With a disappointed shrug, Guy began to retrace his steps in the direction of the car.

He would have liked to have gone deeper into Richmond's activities — into his house itself, even; but although it was almost dark, there was a chance that the track was under observation, in which case to approach the other house without good excuse might lead him into more trouble than he was prepared to face until he knew what plot, if any, he was up against.

The temptation to have a look at Richmond and find out for certain if he was Craig Tyler was strong, but Guy suppressed it for the moment in favour of putting through a phone call in connection with the registration number of the car he had seen. It might throw quite a lot of light not only on Richmond himself, but on his activities as well, if Guy knew who his visitor had been.

Finding a telephone was the most pressing need of the moment, and afterwards he made up his mind to come back to Fortune Cay and enter it somehow or other under cover of darkness. If he drew blank inside the cottage as to the source of the mystery, he would spy out the land in a different direction the next morning, possibly finding some vantage point from which he could watch Pardoner's Folly at close quarters.

One sight of the man Richmond would be enough to tell him if he was or was not the supposedly dead Craig Tyler, and that would settle once and for all the question of whether Guy was really on the track of anything within the scope of his calling.

In his heart Guy rather hoped that

Tyler would prove to be very much alive. More than once in the past their paths had crossed, and each time the enmity between them had grown. There were scores to settle on both sides, and Tyler could hardly live a charmed life forever. Guy was conscious of a tingle of anticipatory thrill at the promise of his thoughts, for he was fully aware that joining battle with a man of Tyler's calibre spelled trouble indeed, and to spare.

Reaching the hollow where the car was concealed, he started up and nosed the long machine across the rough ground and onto the track. Lighting a cigarette with one hand and steering with the other, he set the motor at the first of a series of bends on the way back to the main road. He drove slowly, turning things over in his mind as he went. A vague worry was nagging inside him as to the reason for Mersey's sudden departure from Fortune Cay. He wondered if it really was some private matter, or something else. And 'June'? Apparently expected, whoever she might be. Possibly Mersey's girlfriend, though from Sir Randolph's description of the man Guy was faintly surprised to think him the type to entertain women in this godforsaken spot. All the same, the 'make yourself at home' was certainly suggestive of an amorous interlude. Obviously the intended recipient must have a key to the door, since both the front and back doors had been locked.

Suddenly he remembered that the note was still in his pocket. With a slight feeling of guilt, he wondered if he should return and pin it back on the door for 'June' to see, but on second thought decided she would walk in anyway.

No, he decided, the sooner he reached the village the better. Pressing his foot down on the accelerator, Guy pushed the speed of the car higher, revelling in the increased flick of the wind past his face. He must be near the main road by now, and moving his fingers across the dashboard, he closed the headlight switch to send a twin beam of brilliant white carving through the gloom. Another sweeping bend lay ahead, and with the tyres chucking pebbles against the mudguards in a staccato rattle of sound, he swung the wheel over, swooped up to the next brow, and descended the hill beyond with the speed of a lift.

One more curve, if his memory served him right, and then the road. The uneven surface of the track set the wheel jerking madly in his hands as if it sought to escape his controlling grasp. With a grim smile of pleasure playing at the corners of his mouth, Guy steadied it and put the car at the last bend.

Round came the beam of the lights; dry sedge grass sprang into vivid relief along the verge; shadow stripped bare of shadow gave place to stark grey rock. Following the cloven path of the lights, he edged the motor further over, gave a touch on the brakes, snicked into a lower gear with lightning speed, and began to straighten out.

Perfect cornering, he thought, supremely indifferent to any form of modesty. *If only half the drivers on the ...* And then instantaneously the smile left his lips. His foot slammed down on the brake pedal with urgent pressure; one lean arm shot out to seize the handbrake. For a split second the great car rocked as he fought to hold it, then slithered to a standstill on locked wheels.

In a moment the man was over the side, running forward into the shimmering pool of light with breathless haste, his shadow flung out ahead in an elongated caricature of a human silhouette.

3

The rays of the sun had already begun to climb down the sky by the time June Mersey steered her little two-seater clear of the Scarborough traffic. Even driving as fast as she could, it would be almost dark before she reached Fortune Cay, she thought. Not that it would matter, or make any difference really. Red would know she was coming because of her telegram — if they ever delivered such things in that desolate spot — and anyway her brother was quite used to her blowing in for a night now and then unheralded.

Good sort, Red — she always called her brother that because of his hair — best brother a woman could have. She rather wished he lived somewhere nearer though, or at any rate in a less inaccessible place. Solitude was all very well, she supposed, but it meant she had to go traipsing across that shocking farm track affair every time she wanted to see him. Once she was there, however, she loved the cottage. The wonderful hours they'd spend beating up and down the coast in the sailing dinghy would be fun; so, too, would be the long walks. You could go for miles without seeing a living thing apart from Regan trotting on ahead, nosing into every bush in the hope of setting up a rabbit.

She wondered how Regan was behaving. Red hadn't mentioned him in his last letter — come to think of it, she'd only received one short note from him in the past month. Funny. Still, maybe he was extra busy.

June steered with care round a lumbering lorry. No sense in hurrying and breaking something, she decided. She remembered with annoyance the bumpy moorland track she must use, and slowed down as she approached the turning. Skilfully picking her way over the smoothest part of the churned-up, sun-baked surface, she set the little car at the slope. It would take the best part of half an hour at this rate, but it couldn't be helped.

Her eyes, being fixed on the road a few yards ahead, failed to see the rising plume of dust that peeped coyly from the crest of the next hill. So intent was she on her careful pathfinding, in fact, that the first inkling she received of disaster to come was the strident blaring of a horn clamouring for right of way. Looking up with horror-stricken eyes, she saw the ugly bulk of an enormous saloon bearing down on her. On and on it came without slackening speed, demanding her by imperious blasts to pull over.

The little car was almost at a standstill, and desperately she spun the wheel to the left. Seeing her action, the driver of the saloon accelerated, hooting furiously at the same time; and, as June's front tyres bounced over the verge, he crowded past, catching the rear of the other car a glancing blow with his bumper.

June gave a cry of dismay as the near wheels went into the ditch on the other side of the verge with a sickening thud. She felt herself sliding helplessly from her seat as the car reared up above her. For seconds she seemed to hang in the air; and then, with a bang that knocked the wind from her body, she hit the bracken, to find herself pressed face down by an almost unbearable weight across her shoulders.

* * *

A dozen noises separated themselves. June's ears caught the *glug-glug* of petrol draining from the inverted tank; the sharp tick of contracting metal as the silencer cooled; a final squeaky crack from the distorted windscreen. She noticed dazedly that the dashboard clock was still going, and wondered if she was injured. A furious hate flamed up inside her against the driver of the saloon — she could hear the sound of his engine rapidly fading in the distance. Road hog!

She might have to wait for ages before someone came along. All night perhaps. Heavens, what a mess! She tried a tentative wriggle. No bones appeared to be broken, which was encouraging.

Warm oil dripped monotonously onto her thighs from the gearbox, seeping uncomfortably through the thin material of her summer dress. She swore a little. It gave her an odd feeling of satisfaction. She ought

27

to be thankful it was no worse, but instead began to cry very quietly, the tears falling softly to make inconsequential patterns in a sticky pool of engine oil among the leaves. Fool! What good would it do to cry?

She sniffed noisily, then sniffed again with a curious tightening inside her. Her pulse quickened. Something ... All at once her heart was pounding in her throat. The horrible, unmistakeable smell of burning rubber came to her. Short hairs at the nape of her neck crawled icily; a deadly fear seized her.

She must get clear! She must! Oh, God! To be burned alive, trapped and helpless! Anything — anything but that! She was pleading; begging. Frantically she tried to wrench herself free of the oppressive weight. Panic choked her as the scent of coming torture lightly teased her nostrils for the second time.

Sobbing with blind, unreasoning ter-ror, she fought and struggled in vain. She kicked out with her legs; tore at the earth beneath until her fingers broke and bled; screamed into the mocking, silently lovely evening; and then, from the corner of her red-rimmed, staring eyes, she saw a faint tendril of smoke, followed an instant later by a spark of yellow glowing fire.

For some reason she never understood, the sight of it cleared her mind. Here was the last chance ever to be offered if she was to go on living. Holding grimly to the thin edge of Sanity, she tried to think.

The steering wheel of the car pinned her firmly to the ground, but her arms were free, and somewhere above her, on the floor between the seats, was a Pyrene. It almost dislocated her shoulder to reach it, but at last with trembling fingers she felt the cold, cylindrical shape. Freeing it from the clip by a painful effort, she turned the handle, pulled out the plunger, and, pressing it against her side, sent a jet of liquid as near as she could judge towards the centre of the ominous glow behind the dashboard. A furious sizzling noise rewarded her, and repeating the performance, she scored another hit.

Smoke and fumes made her cough, and brought scalding tears to her eyes, but the fire was no longer burning. The red-hot wires grew black and dead; the battery shorted into impotence.

A wave of reactionary exhaustion swept over the woman; her head flopped forward and her body went limp. Even the pressure between her shoulders seemed to dull and recede. A yawning gulf of Infinite Night stretched out below her, beckoning on with tempting fingers. Slowly at first, then more rapidly, she slipped further and further into the abyss, until in the end she was careering madly downwards; falling ... falling ... falling.

★   ★   ★

All Guy could see as he raced across the short distance between his own car and the overturned two-seater was a pair of very still, very dirty, silk-stockinged legs protruding from under the wreckage. A thin wisp of acrid smoke hung in the air, but as far as he could make out there was no sign of fire to go with it.

How the little car had come to grief he could hazard no guess, but whatever the cause might be he must find out if the owner of the legs was alive. Hurrying round to the opposite side, he looked underneath. A slim, grimy hand rested limply in the bracken, and reaching in he touched it with his fingers. It was wet with oil, but warm.

Guy ran back to his own car, returning a moment later armed with the jack. Adjusting it between the top edge of the car body and the ground, he slowly raised the weight a few inches; then, grasping the two legs firmly about their respective ankles, he eased their owner from underneath in cautious movements. Stooping down, he gathered the slender, crumpled form in his arms, and, with no apparent effort, carried her back to the Bentley. He laid her gently across the front seats, and, putting on the dash-lamp, directed its glow downwards.

The first clear view he had of the woman brought a wave of compassion over him. She was alive all right, and when he put an ear below her breast the beating of her heart sounded steady, but she was pitifully bedraggled.

'Poor thing,' he muttered. 'You are in a mess!' Her long dark hair might well have been one matted tangle, so thickly was it caked with mould and oil. Smudges covered her face, while a tiny spider crawled adventurously down the delicate curve of her throat. Her pale green dress was stained and torn raggedly open from collar to belt. Guy brushed the trespassing spider away and cushioned the woman's head on his knee, then reached for a flask tucked into the door pocket beside him. Pulling down her lower lip with his finger, he let some of the brandy trickle between her teeth, and watched with a satisfied smile as she choked a little, then flickered her eyelids.

Quickly he checked for broken bones or external injury, but she was remarkably unharmed, considering what she had experienced. When he was through, he looked again at her face, to meet a wide-eyed stare; brown eyes gazed into his own, half in fear, half in wonderment, like a child waking from a troubled dream.

'You're quite safe,' he said soothingly. 'A little shop-soiled, I'm afraid, but otherwise undamaged, as far as I can tell.'

The woman moved her head as if not understanding.

'Better take it in easy stages,' he advised. 'Try everything carefully first to see if it works.'

She closed her eyes for a few moments, and Guy saw they were clearer when she reopened them. His arm gave her solid support; and, still without speaking, dreamily, dazedly, she raised her hand, twisted one arm, bent first her left leg then her right. Guy put forward a hand to help as she pressed against his shoulder in an effort to sit up.

Leaning back against the seat squab, she looked at him in a puzzled way. 'Red,' she whispered. 'You're not Red — you're not a bit like him. How did I get here? I was asleep, and why am I so dirty?' She broke off, pushing away the flask he offered. 'I'm all right.' Her look grew suspicious. 'Who are you?' Suddenly realising the state of her torn dress, she gave him a frightened glance, and hastily pulled it across her chest to cover the pink of a satin slip beneath.

Guy sat back in his seat with an inward smile. He really believed she thought she was the victim of an assault. As he watched, she began to rub some of the filth from her arms and legs. Her movements were easy now, and her composure seemed to have fully returned. Guy was intrigued by the complete lack of normal reactions he would have expected her to show after coming to as she had done, but thought it better not to rush her in any way. Really, he supposed, he ought to take her straight to a doctor, but first of all he wanted to know more about her, for had she not been using the track at the time of the accident? And, as Guy had decided before, anyone who did that was of interest.

'Feeling better now?' he asked at length.

She nodded dully; then: 'I just don't understand anything.'

Guy was thinking rapidly. It seemed that her memory had been impaired by shock, yet she spoke of 'Red'. Using the track as she had been doing, she must have been on her way either to Fortune Cay or Pardoner's Folly, since it led nowhere else; and, looking at her covertly, he felt she was hardly the type to favour men like Richmond. Ergo, this dirty, dishevelled, rather frightened woman beside him was in all probability Mersey's pin-up 'June'.

Frankly, he admired the man's taste. Straightened out and washed, he recognised the fact that she would be remarkably attractive. If he played his hand wisely, this waif of circumstance might well prove to be an ace card. To begin with, if she *was* June, she could provide him with a means of entry to the deserted cottage. And in whichever direction she led him, the going was likely to be interesting to say the least.

The question was, which camp did she belong to? He must settle that once and for all in his mind before going any further. Impressions were deceptive, and however certain he was that she had nothing to do with Richmond, he must make quite sure. An ally — even the woman — would be valuable, but if she turned out to be a potential enemy things might become awkward. If, however, she was suffering from amnesia, even discovering salient facts would be easier said than done. 'Red' was about the only clue he had to work on, apart from the woman herself.

'You had an accident,' he explained gently. 'That's why you're in such a mess.'

'Accident? What sort?' She sounded

surprised, or doubtful; he wasn't sure which.

'Car crash. I found you underneath a little two-seater over there.' He pointed to where the beam of the headlights illuminated the chassis and wheels of the overturned motor. 'Heaven knows why it didn't catch fire — there was a good old rubbery smell when I arrived on the scene.'

He paused to see the effect of his words. The woman shivered as she looked at him, horror dawning in her eyes. 'You mean I might have been burnt alive?'

'Could have been, but you were unconscious, so maybe you wouldn't have known much about it.' He meant it to sound consoling.

Her hand went up to her forehead. 'I'm terrified of fire. It's the one thing I'm really scared of; but it's funny I can't remember a thing about it.'

'If you can remember that, it's something.'

With a puzzled expression she examined her fingers, which were blood-caked and sore. Guy daubed them with a liberal dose of iodine, and when its sting failed to draw more than a slight wince from her, she went up several points in his estimation. Without question or comment, she allowed him to bind the worst of her cuts with sticking plasters, and only when he was finished did she thank him in a somewhat dubious voice.

Having tended her in this way, Guy set about the task of helping her to rediscover her identity and, what was more important from his own point of view, her possible connection with either Fortune Cay or Pardoner's Folly. 'Who's Red?' he probed.

'Red? I ... I ...' She hesitated, frowning. 'I don't know. Ought I to ...'

Guy swung his legs to the ground, faintly impatient. It looked as if he was in for an uphill battle, and no mistake. 'Have you the ghost of an idea as to who you are?' He made his voice as reasonable as he could, but the blank stare of the woman was no reward. 'You must have had a handbag or something with you,' he said. 'I'm going to look in your car.'

The idea brought a trace of interest to her eyes. 'I'll come with you. There's nothing wrong with me.'

Except that you don't even know who you are, thought Guy rather bitterly as he held out a steadying hand. She climbed down beside him, self-consciously holding her torn dress together. Opening the tool-box on the running board, Guy rummaged inside. 'Here you are,' he said, producing a length of flex. 'Tie yourself together with this if you're shy.'

Gratefully she took the wire, and moving away from him, fumbled about while he waited. A moment later she turned. 'Ready,' came the simple announcement. She avoided his hand and walked beside him, hurrying a little to keep up.

Lying on his face, Guy felt about in the space beneath the car. A fire extinguisher rolled out, followed presently by a small handbag which he found in a fold of the canvas hood. 'Might be something here,' he said. 'Let's have a look, shall we?' This time she made no attempt to avoid his friendly supporting arm.

Back in the front seat of the Bentley, he undid the bag and tipped the contents out so that they fell in a heap on the lap of her dress. The usual collection of useful and useless articles lay before him: loose change, four pounds in notes, keys, bus tickets, hair grips, cleaners' receipts ... Guy sighed. *The stuff women carry about*, he thought exasperatedly. There was also make-up, a fountain pen, a driving licence, and an identity card. He seized on the last two items greedily and sat very still as her name printed itself on his mind. June Mersey, Scarborough address. So she *was* the fabulous 'June'. Not the artist's girlfriend, but better still, his sister.

Eagerly she peered over his shoulder, waiting for him to speak, but instead of saying anything he passed the evidence to her in silence, and arranged facts in his mind. Now that he knew who she was, he felt justified in telling her things; things that might break down the barrier that encircled her brain — a brain he felt sure would open fresh avenues of knowledge if he could learn what it held.

'I can tell you a little more than those will,' he said quietly. 'When I found you, you were on your way to a cottage by the sea named Fortune Cay — mean anything?' His eyebrows made the question, but her response was negative. Undeterred by this initial failure, he went on: 'If my guess is correct, you're the sister of an artist called Peter Mersey — you could be his wife of course, but I don't think he's married, and anyway you wear no ring, so I favour the sister angle.' The woman nodded understandingly as he continued: 'Since none of this appears to mean much to you, I suggest we carry on from where you left off and go to Fortune Cay. You're expected, by the way,' he added, remembering the note in his pocket. Pulling it out, he showed it to her in the hope that perhaps the handwriting might give her a clue, but there again his luck was out. Thrusting it back inside his shirt, he reverted to his previous idea. 'It might help your memory,' he said, 'if you saw and handled familiar things.'

She raised no objection, and he breathed a sigh of relief as he saw that he was as good as inside Mersey's home already. The phone call regarding the car number would have to be shelved for the moment. With a golden opportunity playing into his hands like this, he intended to seize it and make the very most of it.

As he spoke, he brought the engine to life and began backing the car to turn on a level patch of ground. He was surprised to find the woman taking everything so much for granted, but supposed her somewhat exasperating manner was to be expected in view of her loss of memory. Whether he liked the idea or not, he knew he would have to free himself of her unless her memory returned very soon, and he hoped that her association with the cottage would bring about some useful result.

With June settling in beside him, Guy gave the winding track the respect and attention it deserved; but when he reached the crest from which he had seen the American saloon he slipped into neutral, cut the lights, and coasted the big car ghostlike down the slope to Fortune Cay. Chary of announcing his arrival by the throaty roar of the exhaust, he fell back again on the naturally secretive streak in his character — for he had no desire that Richmond should know of his presence at the cottage — and pulled up quietly some distance away, the car concealed by a copse of densely growing trees.

Swinging to the ground, he turned to assist June. She stood up, opened the door of the car, put one foot to the running board, and was about to join him when she slipped on the worn ribbing of the step mat. Guy's arm shot out to save her, but before he could prevent it her shoulder came down heavily on the horn button. The silence he had sought so carefully to preserve was split and shattered irrevocably by two seconds of blaring sound. That strident blast of noise, he knew, would have been audible for miles around in the still night air.

'Oh dear,' June said, abashed. With a little more roughness than he intended, Guy led her to the cottage door, and, taking the keys from her shaky fingers, tried several until the latch clicked back and they were free to walk across the threshold. On the point of entering, he noticed her hesitate.

'Let's go,' he said. 'You have more right to enter than I have, I promise you.'

'It all seems so strange,' she muttered, and the troubled sound of her voice made him relent. He heard her take a deep breath like a swimmer about to plunge into cold water; then before he could check her, she stepped in front of him with a defiant gesture, and, without waiting, disappeared into the dark interior of Fortune Cay.

Guy swore quietly to himself; he had not intended her to go ahead of him into the darkness like that. He was perhaps eighteen inches behind her, drawing a flash-lamp from his pocket, when he heard her utter a choking cry. His blood ran cold as he sprang forward, shining the lamp in front of him.

On the other side of the room something moved; something that slithered across the floor with an uncanny scuffling sound.

4

Guy grabbed June's hand and edged out backwards through the door with her, whipping out his gun while he continued to shine the beam of the flash-lamp into the fear-laden darkness ahead. Sweeping it to and fro in an endeavour to see what dread thing the shadows might hold, he stiffened suddenly. Beneath the heavy table in the centre of the room was a still form. It was a man clad in grey overalls supporting his weight on his elbows, and staring into the light with unblinking malevolent eyes. A wide mouth curled in a soundless snarl as pain contorted his features.

Guy cast a glance at the horror-struck June, then took a step further into the room. The man's hands were empty, and obviously he was injured in some way, so there was no fear of an attack. Bending down warily, Guy watched as the man made a movement in the direction of the door. He pulled himself along by his arms, and the lower part of his body dragged as if it had no power of its own. The sight of a long-handled knife protruding from his back just above the waist told Guy the reason. There was something horrible yet fascinating in his progress, and Guy found himself held silent as the man moved again, inch by inch, towards where he stood.

Striving to break the spell that bound him, Guy opened his mouth to speak, but before he could utter a word the man's head fell forward, his hands clawed convulsively for a moment, and all movement ceased as he lay still.

For a second Guy remained rigid. Then, shaking off a senseless repulsion, he bent close to the inert figure, and, taking one stiff, hairy wrist between his fingers, felt for a pulse. The man was stone dead.

He straightened up, a dozen questions chasing one another unanswered through his brain. The deeper he became entangled in this business, the more complicated and involved it seemed to grow. First Mersey's letter to Sir Randolph with that half-promise in the last sentence, then the deserted cottage. June with her maddeningly blank mind, and now ... this, with the sinister shadow of Richmond always hovering in the background. And the key to it all — in Fortune Cay itself? Guy was sure of it.

He looked at the dead man more closely, wondering how he came to be there; for when he had peered through the windows on his first visit, the place had most certainly been empty. The man must have entered in some way since then; but how, if that was the case, had he met his fate? And what had that fate been? If sudden death lurked within the four walls of Fortune Cay, Guy wanted to know whence it came. Where one man could die, so could another, and he had no intention of joining the body on the floor.

Warily he switched off his torch, then closed both the kitchen door and that at the foot of the stairs. Going outside again, he approached June. She looked at him dazedly.

'I'm going to take you inside,' he said. 'There's nothing to be scared of — he's dead. Stay with me and you'll be all right.'

She nodded blankly without speaking, but hung back as he moved to the door, following him with obvious reluctance. Closing it behind them, he led her gently to a chair. Then, still in the dark, he took the tablecloth and spread it over the corpse. Deciding that more could be achieved if they had some light on the subject, he drew the heavy curtains across the windows and, fumbling with the unfamiliar gas fittings, lit one of the two brackets above the fireplace.

June caught her breath when she saw the ominously sheeted man on the floor, but much to Guy's relief remained calm. Pleased as he was by this fact, he had nevertheless begun to wonder if she would be more of a hindrance than a help to him now. He was by no means a sentimentalist, but as he gazed at the lovely, vulnerable young woman, an innate friendliness in his nature now reared its head, and prompted him to do all he could to help her.

'I'm going over this place with a fine-toothed comb,' he said. 'Will you be all right here?'

'With that?' She pointed nervously to the corpse.

'He can't hurt you.'

'I'd rather come with you — if I won't be in the way.'

Guy nodded. 'Come on then.' It was a grudging consent.

The kitchen came under examination first. It boasted no cover of any sort where a man might hide, and the door to the back garden was locked on the inside with the key still in position, so nobody could have entered from that direction. A stone floor echoed their footsteps dully, and beside the little sink was a pile of dirty plates. Guy frowned. Mersey must have been called away in a great hurry to have left such signs, for certainly he was not normally an untidy man if the state of the lounge was any indication. Greatly puzzled, he led the way upstairs, treading with care and holding his gun before him.

Two small bedrooms, tastefully furnished and decorated, occupied the upper floor. One was obviously Mersey's, while in the other were some articles of female attire hanging on the back of the door. June's, thought Guy, making a guess. She showed no sign of recognition, however, and disappointedly he went on with his search.

Prying into every conceivable hiding place, he found nothing suspicious, apart from the fact that Mersey's bed was unmade — further evidence of the haste with which the man had departed. Feeling strangely defeated, Guy went downstairs, followed by June.

'I don't know what it's all about,' she said, looking at him when they were once more in the lighted lounge. 'But I wish I could help.' Her eyes were trustful now, holding no malice.

'So do I,' he said. He still had a feeling that if only he could break down the door that barred her mind from his own, he would be halfway to solving the riddle of Fortune Cay. He wished he was a brain doctor; there must be some way of unlocking that nebulous barrier. In all his previous experience, this was something against which he had never been pitted.

'Please,' he urged her. 'Please, try to remember. You may be the possessor of some very important information. You must be able to recall *something*, surely?'

'No, I can't!' she suddenly flared. 'I can't

remember anything!' Tears of frustration began to prick the corners of her eyes.

'All right, June,' Guy said very quietly. 'But look — murder has been done here; murder may still be done. This cottage contains some secret, and I'm going to get to the bottom of it no matter what I do. The owner knows something, but he isn't here. You're his sister, though, and I believe you could tell me as much as he could. It's a hunch I've got — intuition, if you like — but whatever it is, I can feel it. We have simply *got* to find a way of restoring your memory.'

With a sigh and a shake of his head, he walked to the fireplace and gazed moodily at the shape under the tablecloth. How in the name of the devil had the man got in here? he wondered for the hundredth time. He knelt beside the body, pulled back the tablecloth, and ran his hands over its clothing. There was not so much as a tram ticket or a box of matches in the half-dozen pockets. No marks on the clothes; no name; nothing at all. Blank again, in fact.

Guy stood up after rearranging the cloth as a shroud. Not until then did he realise that June was crying in full now, the tears coursing down her wet cheeks. Again he felt that wave of compassion and pity which had swept over him at first sight of her, and going quickly over to her, he took her hands in his own.

'I'm sorry, my dear,' he said, all his previous annoyance gone. 'Please try to forgive me — even if I don't deserve it.'

She raised her eyes, which were misted and troubled. 'I feel awful,' was all she said.

'You might feel better if you exchanged those ripped clothes for something else. There are some upstairs ... your own, I think.'

She shuddered. 'I couldn't go up there alone.' Her eyes seemed drawn to the shape by the table. 'Will you come with me?'

'I'll wait outside the door, if you like,' he replied. 'Here's the torch.'

She took it from his hand rather unsteadily and led the way up, flashing it as she went. Entering the bedroom, she left the door half-open, and Guy leaned against the framework, smoking and thinking.

Despite his conviction that the secret lay within the cottage itself, he had so far learned practically nothing. The body of the man downstairs might be of some assistance when it was identified, but to have that done would mean bringing the police into it, and if he could find out more without them, so much the better. As soon as June was ready, he decided, he would drive to the village, find a phone, and leave her somewhere in safety until the affair was over. Perhaps the number of the American saloon would lead him on a more profitable track. He still disliked the idea of quitting the place, however; something seemed to hold him there, almost against his will — and certainly now, against his better judgment.

Fortune Cay. The very name haunted his thoughts. Savagely, he ground out his half-burnt cigarette. If only the body below could speak! Or June, for that matter.

'How are you getting on?' he called.

'I'm only half-dressed,' came her voice in answer.

'All right,' he said, 'but hurry. We're going motoring again.'

A few moments later, as he waited, he heard her moving about, and then she was beside him on the landing, neatly dressed in a woollen sweater and slacks and looking far more presentable than when he had last seen her. Still holding the torch in one hand, he noticed she carried her torn clothes in the other.

'Shall I take those?' he offered when they were at the head of the stairs.

She half-turned towards him, a smile on her face as it caught the light from below. 'Thank you,' she said.

He gave her a friendly grin as he took the bundle from her hands. 'We mustn't waste time now. The important thing is to get you fixed up somewhere for the time being.'

Her fingers touched the bannister rail; and then, before Guy realised what was happening, he felt the clothing jerked sharply from his arm, heard a cry of alarm from June, and saw her topple on the edge of the first step. Too late, he reached out to catch her, and a second later she pitched head foremost down the stairway, to land at the bottom in a still, silent huddle of arms and legs, the length of flex from her torn dress coiled in a snake-like tangle round her ankle.

5

'Damn and blast!' said Guy as he leapt down the stairs in her wake. He hoped he was not going to have another corpse on his hands — the place would become overcrowded. No, he decided as he bent over her, she was alive, but well and truly out for the count. A thin trickle of blood welled from a superficial cut on her forehead. Lifting her up, he carried the slender form to one of the deep armchairs and lowered her into it with care, and not a small amount of guilt.

He had to admit that this latest mishap was hardly her own fault, as he himself had supplied her with the flex with which she had become entangled; but however sorry he might feel about it, he realised that he really must find someplace to drop her off so that he could continue his investigation on his own, without hindrance. Carefully considering things, he came to the conclusion that the most sensible course of action would be to put her in the car and drive her straight to the village, which would fit in at the same time with his previous plan to find a phone box.

Turning out the gas and picking June up again, Guy opened the door and placed her comfortably in the Bentley with a folded coat beneath her head. Careless now of making any noise, he woke the engine to a crackling roar, and letting in the clutch, jockeyed the great car thunderously up the first mile of climbing track.

As soon as the first crest was behind him he dropped the speed, partly to save jolting the unconscious woman beside him, and partly to give himself time to think. It was obvious that there were going to be plenty of awkward questions flying about when the body in the cottage was discovered, and in his unofficial status things might be tricky. In the possible event of his movements being traced, he might easily be suspected of murder, and knew only too well that under no circumstance was he permitted to fall back on his real position as a cover against police investigation.

June, too, might be suspect. There was

her overturned car, and her torn clothes left in the cottage; and now it looked as if he was being forced to bring her out into the open. How, then, would he explain his own presence on the only road to Fortune Cay? He could hardly just leave her on the local constable's doorstep, and in any case his car was sure to be seen or heard by someone in the village. If only she hadn't fallen downstairs! That was the worst possible luck, for had she been conscious he could have left her in the village without himself coming into the picture at all. He shrugged. A solution would come to him eventually, and meanwhile he was going to make sure of that phone call.

Guy continued driving, steadily and carefully. The still form of June at his side gave him much food for thought. At odd moments since he had first found her, she had shown qualities he liked, though on the whole her actions, and even her speech, had been dulled and flattened by shock. Normally, he decided, she would probably be an intelligent, engaging person, as well as being unusually attractive. He glanced at her pale face, trying to picture it as the everyday world must have done before tonight. He made guesses at her occupation, her likes and dislikes, and the way she laughed. These things and many others drifted through his mind, and by the time they reached the main road he was wishing he knew more about her.

With a good road surface beneath its wheels, the car ran smoothly, so that Guy was able to push the speed up until the tempest of their progress throbbed in his ears like a mad concerto of buffeting sound — exhilarating, stimulating, yet forming as well an escape from his thoughts. He steered lightly, almost carelessly enjoying the brief indulgence in speed for the love of the thing. Not until the wide beam of the headlights sent back dancing stars of reflection from a shop window did he ease his foot off the throttle and bring the exhaust to an idle rumble of low-pitched sound.

The village pressed against the road on either side, an ugly man-made sprawl of houses. There were harsh edges of dull brickwork, grey stone walls, dusty hoardings, and here and there a sentinel lamp-post. The short journey was over all too soon, and Guy came back to earth, his eyes searching for the familiar red of a wayside phone box.

Almost in the centre of the place he found what he sought. Near a stagnant horse trough he pulled up, and climbing down, entered the small glass-panelled booth. He dialled the exchange and waited patiently, his mind busy with what he should say when he was through to London. The sources of information he could tap would provide him with whatever he wanted to know — Sir Randolph's organisation was thorough and far reaching — but it would mean waiting some hours for it; and there was the difficulty of June to be faced.

When at last the operator put him through, Guy spoke to a quiet, impersonal voice. He gave the number of the car and asked to know the name of the owner, as well as brief details concerning him. It was entirely unnecessary, he knew, to say that it was urgent — these men dealt with every enquiry as if someone's life depended on it, as indeed it often did — and contented himself with asking when he could expect a reply.

The voice informed him that the name would be available within an hour but that the rest might take as much as a day to collect and tabulate. Guy glanced through the glass at June in the car. He'd have to keep her with him for another hour at the very least. 'I'll ring you back then,' he said into the mouthpiece, checking the time with his listener.

He was rather surprised to find when he looked at his watch that it was barely midnight. Fortunately the village was sleeping soundly, or curious eyes might have wondered why a woman in a car should sit so still. Better slip out into the country for the next hour, he decided, and surely by then she would have come round, so that, even now, he might save himself the awkwardness of coming out into the open.

Satisfied with the arrangement, Guy drove slowly through the straggling cluster of houses until finally they thinned and gave way to open common land, with here and there the darker patch of a forestry plantation. Drawing into the shadow of one of these where it ran down to the road, he switched off the engine and sat still for a moment in the sudden hush of silence. A faint wink of starlight filtered through the black tracery of needle leaves above, while somewhere in the far distance his ears caught the eerie hoot of an owl.

A man of quickly changing moods, Guy found himself wedded to the mysterious vastness of Night. He needed no company; no live, vital being to jar and interrupt this strangely sensuous love into the arms of whose spell he gave himself. The darkness itself, the tiny whispers of the earth and trees: they were sufficient. For long minutes he surrendered to this intangible caress, then suddenly shook himself free of its opiate grip.

Present problems must be faced and untangled; fresh moves worked out and clarified. Like the shadow of a storm cloud, his mind hovered over the thought of Richmond: limping, dangerous, wholly mysterious, a figure of menace standing always just beyond his reach. Behind a dead man on a cottage floor? Guy was sure of it. Behind the seemingly too-hasty departure of Peter Mersey? Of that he was not so certain, but in his thoughts the doors and roof of Fortune Cay, its whole material existence in fact, was inextricably linked with the name of Richmond. A cottage floor. Whichever way his thoughts ran, they always came back to that desolate cliff top, haunt of seabirds, mystery, and — death.

Mechanically he lit a cigarette, left the car, and walked up and down the road. The air was clean; the ghost of a breeze played icy fingers across his face. For perhaps fifty yards he strolled slowly, then turned and began to retrace his steps.

He was ten paces from the car when he heard a sound that was no part of his passing reverie. It came from the Bentley, and was an unmistakable moan. Guy broke into a run, and, putting on the dash-lamp, saw that June was moving. She passed a hand over her eyes, felt her head gingerly, then licked her lips. A second groan, louder and more urgent than he first, pressed Guy to hurried action, and reaching out he lifted her head slightly and held the flask of brandy to her mouth.

'Have some of this,' he offered persuasively. 'It'll do you good.'

'Thanks,' she said at last. The act of

speaking seemed to cause her pain. 'I wish my head didn't ache so.'

'You gave it a nasty crack when you fell downstairs,' he said kindly.

She sat upright in her seat, startled by his words, puzzled, frowning. 'But … but the car was on fire!' She was excited now. 'And my clothes — they're different! What's been happening to me?' It was both a question and an accusation.

Guy grew very still. A touch of incredulity teased his brain, to be thrust aside in an instantaneous wave of relief as the full realisation of what had happened dawned on him.

June's memory had returned. Accident had succeeded where he himself had failed. The rather satanic lines of his face became gay with an inward laughter; a laughter that held more than mere pleasure. Now, he thought elatedly, many things would become clear; many questions had only to be asked to be answered. With her brain once more the source of intelligence it normally was, he would soon be a far wiser man.

'Bless you, woman,' he said, and his voice was gentle with a deeper note of tenderness than he had meant it to hold.

The half-hour that followed was crowded. Guy redressed the cut on her forehead, produced sandwiches from the back of the car, and added a pint bottle of beer and a thermos flask of coffee which they shared. While they ate and drank, he told her all that had happened since the moment he'd come upon her beneath the upturned two-seater. Nothing was omitted. It was a bitter disappointment to Guy, however, when after numerous questions, he found she had no more idea of what her brother had suspected when he wrote to Sir Randolph than he had himself. In fact, she did not even know anything had been wrong at all, but was deeply concerned to hear of his sudden departure from the cottage.

'I can't understand him doing a thing like that.' She frowned. 'I wired him that I was coming, and yesterday morning he rang me up from the village.' She lapsed into silence, and Guy, glancing at his watch, realised that by the time they got back to the phone box, the allotted hour would be up. Turning the car, he began to head back the way he had come.

'This dead man,' said June suddenly. 'You say all the doors were locked?'

Guy nodded. 'Yes. Tight as anything — and he wasn't in the place when I first looked it over.'

'I wonder ...' she said slowly.

Her words were low, so that Guy barely heard, but his head twisted sharply towards her. 'Why do you say that?' It was more a demand than a question, and as he spoke he slowed the car to a crawl.

She hesitated for a moment; then: 'Can I see that note you found on the door?'

He pulled it from his pocket and stopped the car. Holding it under the glow of the dash-lamp, she studied the lines, biting her lip as she did so. Guy waited, his eyes on her face, wondering what was coming. When at last she looked up, her expression was grave.

'There's something terribly wrong somewhere,' she said. 'Never once in his life has my brother signed a letter, or a note, or anything addressed to me with his real name, Peter — always 'Red'. It started as a joke when we were kids — when I was a kid — and stuck ever since.'

'It *is* his handwriting though.' Guy fought hard against a dread that crept up at the back of his mind. The dread of being too late.

'Yes — or a very good imitation.' She was definite on the first syllable, but fear grew up in the sound of the last as its implication dawned on her.

Guy took the paper from her unresisting hand. Was this a clue laid purposely by a man in danger? Or had someone else written it? Someone who knew of her intended visit, and meant to lull any suspicion in her mind at Mersey's absence; someone ignorant of his nickname, and therefore creating an exactly opposite impression? Guy couldn't tell, but was determined to find out. Either solution pointed to Mersey being in some deadly peril; and if Richmond was indeed Craig Tyler, Guy knew just how deadly that peril might be. The man was ruthless; anyone standing in his way could expect no quarter — and Peter Mersey, by the very fact of his presence at Fortune Cay, did just that. His absence took on a far more sinister significance, so that where before it had merely been annoying, it was now something to be looked into with all speed.

'What did you mean when you said 'I wonder' a few minutes ago?' asked Guy.

For several seconds June remained silent, deep in thought. At last: 'I know it sounds fantastic, but there's another way of entering Red's cottage.'

Guy straightened up with a jerk. 'Yes?' he urged, watching her closely.

'In the kitchen,' she explained, 'there's a cellar under the floor, and steps leading down from that to a little cave at sea level. You'd never know it was there unless you were told about it. It's supposed to be some old pirate's secret way of getting in and out of the place. I went down once when Red first discovered it. He only stumbled on it by accident himself. You do something in the kitchen — I can't quite remember what, but it'll come back to me — and one of the big paving stones in the floor swings down.' She stopped, her face eager; and Guy, his blood tingling with unwonted excitement, set the car hurrying once more in the direction of the village.

So that was the riddle of Fortune Cay!

Things became a little clearer in his mind, but though he now felt he knew the reason for Richmond's desire to gain possession of the cottage, he was still in the dark as to why he should want the use of the secret entrance so badly. Very useful, no doubt; but useful for what? Smuggling? It could be that; yet Craig Tyler was no small-time crook to dabble in illicit odds and ends. Whatever game he was playing, it was big.

Guy felt like a man sitting in on a card game with high stakes on the table and no light by which to read his hand. The cards he held were there to read, but until he could see, and until his opponent's face was unmasked, their meaning must remain obscure. A game in the dark, with Peril for an audience, and Death standing ready at each player's elbow — waiting. Would his call to London draw back the curtains? Bring rays of understanding shining down on the board? Turn the cards face uppermost and so reveal — what? Guy did not know.

The road hurried past; hedges, ditches, trees and gateways blurred into an avenue of shadow slanting away on either side of the carpet of white unrolled by the headlights. June sat silent beside him, lower down and further back in her seat. Intent on the road, some instinct told Guy that her eyes were fixed on his darkened face, seeking to read whatever lay hidden behind the hard etching of its features.

Since recovering her memory, she was a different person: clear-headed, eager despite her worry on account of Mersey, even able to find humour in the tale of her misadventures. Guy found time between his deliberations to give her some thought.

She knew little enough about him. His name, yes. The reason for his presence? Certainly not the real reason. He had given her to understand that he wanted to see her brother on confidential business, but his questions and persistence must have opened her eyes to the fact that he was not all he seemed to be. Besides, she was no fool, and he gave her credit for being fairly shrewd and capable of making guesses. Well, let her. It could do no harm, and just now he needed her help in solving the secret of that lonely cliff-top cottage. Meanwhile, she must think what she liked, unless it became politic to explain himself further. It was a matter in which time and circumstance were dictators.

The clock in the low tower of a crouching church proclaimed the hour as Guy brought the car to rest beside the horse trough for the second time that night.

The voice of the man in London had very little to say. No more than a name, but it was one which caused Guy to draw a sharp breath and experience that minute thrill of excitement which always came as the harbinger of great things.

He needed no dossier, carefully drawn up, tabulated, indexed and highly polished, to tell him that Elgin Crossler was a man to be treated with as much caution as a spiteful cobra — and Elgin Crossler had been Richmond's visitor.

6

Very thoughtfully, Guy hung up the receiver and walked slowly back to the car. He barely noticed the way June looked at him as he swung his legs over the side and pressed the starter; in fact he was hardly conscious of her presence, so intense was his preoccupation.

He reached back into his memory for all the facts with which to clothe the name of Elgin Crossler. The man had a reputation all right, and a bad one at that. For years he had sailed close to the wind. His finance deals were enormous and international in extent. Out of every war he made a fortune from just within the law, stepping warily and knowing how far he could go in safety. Apart from precious stone dealing, Guy knew, too, that in England he owned a somewhat disreputable shipping company.

With Crossler in the picture, Guy was now positive that Richmond was indeed his old enemy Craig Tyler, and the pair made a formidable team. The importance of the secret entrance to Fortune Cay took on a new significance. A little cave at the head of a tiny inlet was the sort of asset for which a man like Crossler could find many uses. On a lonely stretch of coast it formed a back door to England through which many things and many people could pass; people who were forbidden the normal ways of entry.

'Where are we going?' June's question woke him to remembrance of the woman beside him.

'Fortune Cay,' he answered, adding: 'Have you remembered how to open that hole in the floor yet?'

'I've an idea Red did something near the old copper in the corner of the kitchen — I couldn't see very clearly. I know exactly where he stood, though; even where his hands were. He laughed when I wanted to do it myself — said he was guarding his secret from nosey parkers!' She smiled faintly in the darkness, but Guy's mouth hardened.

'I hope you can work the trick when we get there,' he said. 'In this secret panel business you're rather like a blind man's dog — and I'm the blind man. I'm relying on you.'

'I'm sure I'll be able to do it.'

Her voice held a note of confidence he found comforting. This woman was something of an enigma to Guy, but he realised he was leaning on her to quite a large extent. Was she fully aware of the fact? he wondered. He turned his head in the rushing night; for a second the lazy grey eyes met brown ones. 'Your brother's life and a lot more besides may depend on it.' Intentionally he made his voice heavy with underlying meaning to ensure that the seriousness of the situation was fully brought home to her.

She gave a little shiver and looked away. 'I know,' she said quietly. 'You don't have to remind me. I don't know what else depends on it, but I do know I'm awfully afraid for Red.' She put a hand impulsively on his arm. 'What do you think may have happened? That note meant something, I'm sure — more than it said. I'm frightened.'

Guy, too, was afraid for Mersey's sake. 'We'll know something definite before long,

I hope,' he said.

The moorland track seemed rougher than ever when he turned off the main road, but using all his skill, he kept the speed high. The wreck of the two-seater lay behind them now, and ahead lay the sheltering crest from which the track ran down to the cottage. This time, however, Guy decided it would be safer not to take the car right down, but instead left it hidden in the hollow he had previously used for the same purpose.

Together they walked the remaining distance, and when they arrived, Guy hurried the last few yards to the door. The key was in his hand and halfway to the lock when he pulled up short in the very act of inserting it. His brain flicked back to a picture of himself carrying the unconscious form of June through the door and putting her in the car. Of one thing he was certain: the door had been left ajar. And now it was closed.

The wind? Hardly strong enough to move the hair on his head, let alone shut a heavy door. But worse was to come.

Where the dead man should have been on the floor, Guy found nothing. The cool white tablecloth lying in a crumpled heap was all the evidence left to show that it had even been there. Apparently others beside himself had come and gone under cover of darkness.

Guy was worried. If it was the murderer who had returned to remove his victim, he must now be aware that someone else knew of the crime. It was reasonable to suppose, therefore, that in order to protect himself he would take steps to close their mouths as effectively as he had done that of the vanished corpse.

June came up beside him. 'What is it?' she asked, puzzled by his immobility.

'I'm not sure, but I don't like it. The body's gone.' His voice was low. 'Come on in.'

She was breathing fast, moving softly as if afraid to wake an echo. He closed the door and led her through to the kitchen. By the light of the torch he located the old copper built into one corner of the room.

'There you are, June.' Instinctively, he whispered. An uncanny quiet brooded over the house, and, as she moved forward, Guy felt his heart beating faster. His fingers tightened on the chequered butt of his automatic. Like a man awaiting the dawn, he watched, keyed up, tense, not so much in preparation for the opening of the secret trap but for what might be revealed in the cellar beneath. *Hurry, hurry,* he thought, conscious again of that strange dread that haunted him.

She stood leaning slightly backwards, her hands stretched out on either side, searching the brickwork. 'Just like this,' she whispered. 'I know exactly because he — Ah!' It was a sharp intake of breath. She twisted quickly to the left, dropping onto one knee. 'Here!'

Guy stepped against her stooping form, then spun round again in a flash as he heard a tiny sound behind his back.

With a small, gritty squeak, the grey stone slab fronting the floor sank downwards, to leave a square of dead black void. In a second Guy was kneeling on the edge, his torch raking down into the inky pit below.

There was disappointingly little to see: a bare brick-walled space, not much over ten feet either way, floored with roughly hewn rock. Narrow stairs led down from the trap through which he peered, while in one corner he made out the first of a series of steps descending into the virgin rock of the floor.

June was at his elbow now, craning her neck to see. He looked up. 'I'd rather you stayed here,' he said.

She shook her head vehemently. 'I'm coming with you.' Her voice held a note of firm determination.

Guy shrugged. So be it; and there might well be as much danger in the silent house as there would be in the darkness beneath it. There seemed to be peril in the very air of the place. He swung his legs through and felt for the stair.

'Be careful,' she whispered.

A moment later they stood side by side in the cellar. The faintest trace of a smell hung in the air, and with a shock Guy realised what it was. The smell that touched his nostrils was that of burnt cordite, the aftermath of a shot being fired in the confined space. Bending to examine the floor, he found a tell-tale smear of blood. Even half-expecting it as he was, the discovery sent a tingle of excitement through his veins. Was it from the missing corpse, or someone else's? Peter Mersey's, for instance?

His flashlight shifted further afield, coming to rest on a glint of metal. June saw it too, and stooping down, picked something off the floor. Fear sat in her eyes as she held out a signet ring.

'Your brother's?' Guy knew the answer before she gave it. So he was too late. Or was he? For Peter Mersey to have left his ring in the cellar, he must have been alive, since rings don't normally fall off a finger. It seemed to Guy that it had been dropped purposely as a clue, but the fact that a shot had recently been fired worried him considerably.

His light moved to the steps in the floor. 'How far down does it go?' he whispered.

'Forty or fifty feet,' came June's hushed reply. She stood against him, glad of his nearness.

'Come on then,' he muttered, 'and keep quiet — I don't know what we're walking into.'

With no handholds in the rock walls, it was treacherous going. For what seemed an endless time, they continued their descent. Once June's shoes made a slight noise and she stopped to remove them.

Without warning the steps ended abruptly, falling away in a six-foot drop to sand and shingle sloping sharply downwards. Guy halted. 'What happens now?' he breathed.

'This is the cave.' June's lips almost touched his ear. 'The entrance gets covered at high tide, forming a sealed-off basin inside. Red knew about the cave, but the bottom of the steps was blocked with boulders when he first found it.'

'Thanks.' Guy sat on the step and dropped down; then, turning, reached up and lifted June down beside him. With crunching footsteps, they moved slowly forward.

Shining his torch round, Guy revealed a fair-sized cavern, the floor of which was covered by still, black water. 'Must be high tide now,' he said.

Suddenly his attention was riveted on the shape of a small dinghy drawn up on the narrow beach away to the left. He heard June give a gasp of recognition as she saw it; and, with a prickle of dread, he made out the still form of a man huddled between the thwarts.

Before he could stop her, June ran forward, her footmarks mingling with others already pressed into the sand. With a sob she knelt beside the boat, and Guy knew then, even before he reached her side, that his search for Peter Mersey had ended the way he had been afraid it would — with Death playing a trump card while Peril laughed quietly as he groped in the dark.

'Red! Oh Red!' June whispered brokenly, taking the limp hand of the man, her head bent forward. For long seconds all else was forgotten.

Guy realised she was hardly conscious of his presence. Very gently he touched her shoulder. 'Please, June.' In the light of the torch he saw her face — clear-cut, finely chiselled, and lined not with grief and panic as he had feared, but with the dawn of hope.

'He's not dead! Oh Guy, he's not dead! Do something! Please try!'

Her words were true enough; Mersey, though unconscious, still lived. Guy carefully lifted him from the boat and laid him on the sand. A rapid examination quickly told him that the man was far gone, but there was a chance that he might be able to speak before he died. He managed to get a drop of brandy down Mersey's throat, and was elated a few seconds later when the heavy eyelids flickered open. He moved the torch so that its light fell on June's face, knowing that if Mersey recognised anything it would be his sister.

'Hello, Red,' she whispered. 'You know me, don't you?' She was pleading more than asking.

The ghost of a smile came over the man's features, and June raised him a little on her arm.

'Can you tell us what happened?' asked Guy. 'Sir Randolph sent me — sorry to find you like this, old man.'

Bending close, he caught the answering words, slow and laboured, with many pauses during which Guy thought he was finished.

'Richmond,' Mersey said. 'I heard him talking to a fat man. I was behind some gorse. It was all about someone called Pedro, and a boat named the *Arrow*. I couldn't understand much. The fat man asked if the kit was ready for loading by Pedro in the cave. Richmond said yes. I should have heard more but I trod on a twig and made a noise. I ran away, but they caught me. Took me to Pardoner's Folly and found June's telegram in my pocket. Made me write a note, but I signed it wrong — you saw that?'

June nodded silently.

'Then they took me to the cottage. In the kitchen I grabbed a knife and fought like the devil. Managed to get one of Richmond's men. Down in the cellar I dropped my ring, but Richmond shot me when I tried to make a breakaway.' He stopped, weak from the effort of talking.

'Can you give me any idea of what's going on?' asked Guy.

Mersey looked at him. 'I think ...' His words came more slowly, and with glazing eyes he turned to June. 'Sorry, kid — look after yourself.' The voice slurred away into a mumble. Peter Mersey twitched, then slumped back lifeless, taking whatever he knew with him.

7

Many times after hearing those tortured words spoken, Guy recalled the odd mixture of his feelings. At one and the same time he was puzzled by what he heard, filled with a cold hatred against the man who had done this dastardly thing, and conscious, too, of June's emotions.

Even though Peter Mersey had spoken, his words only complicated the problem that Guy had to solve, granting him no more than a peep where he had hoped for a full view. He attached no blame for that to Mersey, poor devil. He had been no more than just another unfortunate who had stood in Tyler's way, stumbling on things he was not meant to know about and paying the penalty for curiosity with his life.

Puzzle as he would, Guy could make nothing of the vague allusions the dying man had made to 'Pedro' and 'kit' and the rest of the disjointed recital. True, his earlier suspicions that Tyler wanted the cave for some very important or very profitable reason were now confirmed beyond question, but it was the *reason* Guy sought more than the fact.

One thing was clear: the dead man could give him no further help, so he must start at the other end — at Tyler's house, trying to pick up something there that would lay bare the bones of the mystery. It meant putting his head into the lion's mouth with a vengeance, but as far as he could see, there was no other way. He could, of course, remain in the cave until 'Pedro' arrived, but for all he knew that might not happen for several days. On the other hand, Guy had no fears that he would not come out of Pardoner's Folly again unscathed, and with full knowledge of the set-up at his fingertips if he chose to enter the place. But, lined up against any move he planned to make, there was once again the problem of June to consider.

Heartbroken as she was bound to be after her loss, the matter would require some careful handling, for Guy certainly had no intention of taking her with him into Tyler's lair. Leave her, then, at Fortune

83

Cay? Too risky. Nor in the cave where they now stood; 'Pedro' was enough to put paid to that idea. For a time he wondered what he was going to do with her, but at last he remembered the sheltering hollow in which the Bentley lay hidden. That should be her haven, and there she could await his return.

He looked down at her. She crouched mutely by her dead brother's side, her head bowed, shoulders drooping, the slight body shaken by a tempest of quivering sobs. Gently but firmly, Guy raised her to her feet.

'Come along, my dear,' he said with a tenderness that surprised even himself. 'We've plenty of urgent work to do.' Let her think she was to have some part in avenging her brother. That was the best line to take at the moment, he decided.

She turned to face him, brushing tears from her pale, wet cheeks. Standing there looking down in the dim light between them, Guy watched an incredible change take place as her features seemed to alter in an almost physical way. Shadows grew where before none had been; the lift of her chin became firm and resolute, hardening visibly; and in a second of time she looked older and altogether more mature. Like a soldier after his first baptismal fire, thought Guy wonderingly.

'I'm ready.' She hesitated. 'We'll come back, won't we?' Her eyes moved back to the body of Mersey. How calm she was all at once.

'Yes, we'll come back — afterwards.'

Moving back to the wall below the stairway, Guy lifted her to the bottom step, then scrambled up himself. Climbing was laborious, and, hurrying as he was, they were both glad when the cellar opened up around them, allowing a much-needed pause.

Casting the light round the grim confined space, Guy saw again the dark smear of blood, the dull brick walls, and wooden stairway; all were unchanged. Had it not been for his vivid memory of every intonation in the dying man's voice, their descent into the cave might well have been a passing nightmare.

Fortune Cay stood above their heads, silent and deserted while across the moor in a rambling house was Tyler. Guy had given up referring to him as Richmond, so sure was he of the man's real identity, and he made a wordless vow that this should be their final meeting. A primitive urge seized him; an urge to destroy this man who had so often slipped through his fingers in the past. It must never happen again, and Guy intended to make certain of it in the only way that would stop Tyler's activities forever.

He was perhaps three steps up the wooden stair to the kitchen when his nerves went taut like vibrating piano wires, twanging a danger signal throughout his body. All his plans and hopes, all his certainties and convictions folded back upon themselves, swept into limbo by one indisputably solid fact; a fact against which there was no argument; a fact that momentarily stunned him.

The trapdoor to the outside world was closed. June, still breathing hard from her efforts to keep up during the long climb, came to an abrupt halt behind him. He made a warning gesture with his hand and began to back down the steps again, switching off the light as he did so.

Guy's thoughts were dark and confused as he surveyed the position. Tyler, then, knew of their presence and had pulled an effective trick by allowing them to walk in before trapping them. It was an eventuality that Guy must have been blind not to foresee, but blaming himself was unlikely to help them now. At any moment the square of stone might swing down to let a hail of bullets come through. Guy had no desire to die in a place like this, as easy a sitting target as some defenceless animal in a cage; nor, for that matter, did he want to hear the unpleasant sound of bullets thudding into June's body beside him.

He put a finger on her lips for silence, then led her back to the steps in the floor. No word had so far passed between them — their breathlessness had seen to that — and possibly this saved their lives, though he could not tell. Taking no chances, however, he went down twenty or thirty steps before coming to a halt. Then, turning to June, he explained his actions.

'Is there any way of opening the trap from below?' he asked when he had finished.

'Not that I know of,' she replied in a hesitant whisper.

'Then we're virtually locked in until low

water when the cave mouth clears — is that it?'

She nodded agreement, but said nothing.

'In that case, we'll go down again and find somewhere to lie up in safety — the cellar is nothing but a death-trap, and these steps aren't much better. Come along.'

The remainder of their descent was uneventful, and once again they were standing on the narrow underground beach. With more care this time, Guy examined the sides of the cave, seeking to find some cleft or shelf that would give them cover from prying eyes.

Not until he had almost given up hope did he make out the darker shadow of a hole in the rocky wall about a third of the way round to the right from where they were. There was no sign of any other possible hiding place, so that would have to serve.

The opening looked to be about three or four feet above the present level of the water, and to reach it would mean either wading or swimming, for using the boat would give Tyler a definite indication of where to look for them. Time also was important, since Guy had no idea when a search would be made — as it would be for sure sooner or later; but once inside the hole they would be safely hidden for the time being. If the worst came to the worst, he thought, it would also be a good position, defensible against practically anything short of a full-scale attack.

'You're going to get wet, I'm afraid,' he whispered to June. Then, taking her by the arm, he walked forward into the still water. Its touch struck icy by comparison with the heat of his body, mounting his legs by slow, creeping inches. How deep the basin was, he had no idea, and consequently he moved with wary steps. He heard June gasp a little as the chill reached her stomach. The water grew deeper and deeper, rising above his waist. Suddenly June lost her footing, to vanish with a splash over the edge of some invisible shelf beneath the surface. Almost overbalancing himself in the effort, he pulled her up again; and then, in a few more steps, they were under the small hole he had marked as the only possible refuge in the bare, dark cavern.

Gaining entry to it, however, presented more difficulty than he had anticipated, for now that he was directly beneath it, Guy found himself standing in a deep hollow of the floor so that the water came nearly to his neck. What was worse, he realised to his dismay that the rock wall above overhung to a degree that made climbing out of the question. By stretching upwards on tiptoe, his fingers just touched the lip of the cavity, but there was no handhold large enough to give him the grip he needed for drawing himself into it.

June, swimming now because she could no longer stand without floating off her feet, supported herself on his shoulder, and he realised he would have to lift her high enough to scramble up. Unstable as was his own precarious footing on the submerged floor, even that proved quite a tricky problem; but, leaning back against the wall, he told her to put one foot in his linked hands, and in that manner make use of his body as a crude form of ladder.

Up until now he had been able to keep the torch clear of the water, but with both hands in use he was forced to give it to June for safekeeping. Gripping it in her mouth so as to leave her own hands free, she did as he said; and, as the weight of her body pressed against his fingers, he heaved upwards. For a second it seemed as if she might overbalance and topple back into the water again, but getting one arm into the hole, she lessened the strain and steadied herself.

'Now tense your legs,' Guy whispered, seizing her by the ankles as he spoke. He shifted his grip inch by inch until he was holding her tightly at the knees, and succeeded in raising her still higher from the water. A moment later the weight of her body grew considerably less, and suddenly he was no longer supporting it. The next instant he had to duck as her foot kicked against his face, and she hauled herself clear of his arms to the safety of the hole.

She, at any rate, was out of harm's way. When the light of the torch showed above him, gleaming on her wet face, Guy wondered how on earth he was going to reach her side. She would certainly not be able to pull him up on her own, but by grasping her hands it might be possible to use his feet on the wall and clamber up in that fashion.

He looked up, anxiously gauging the distance. He was beginning to feel wretchedly cold, for though it was high summer, the air in the cave was dank and chill, seeming to freeze the very water itself.

June, lying face down above his head, put out her hands. His own went up to meet them, but hardly had their fingertips touched before he sensed her go taut. One of her hands whipped away from him, and the next instant the light went out and they were plunged into pitch darkness.

In the faintest of whispers, June spoke. Her words were urgent; a disembodied warning in the world of blackness around them: 'The steps, Guy! Someone's coming.'

His head jerked round. A glimmer of light was dancing on the sides of the stairway. Someone was coming down into the cave, and Guy was exposed for anyone to see who happened to cast a light in that direction.

There was only one thing to do. Swearing softly to himself, he sank down into the water until only his nose and the upper part of his head were above the surface. Praying that the ripples caused by his movement would pass unnoticed, he waited tensely as the sound of descending footsteps came to his ears.

With his eyes fixed on the growing oblong of light, he held his gun ready beneath the water. If this was Tyler, he thought, his chance for a final settling might come within the next few minutes; but the distance was too great to risk a shot from the snub-nosed automatic unless his hand was forced by discovery. He hoped June would make no sound to bring attention towards them, and was a little disturbed by the steady drip of water from over his head. Obviously the floor of her hiding place sloped forward, and though she had drawn herself back into its furthest corner, the water from her sodden clothing was running out to find its way once more to the lower level of the basin. He tried to suppress an involuntary shiver that ran through him — and then, almost before he expected it, the light on the stairway suddenly brightened, and he made out the forms of two men as they dropped from the bottom step to the sandy shingle of the little beach.

The light of the torch one held shone on the face of the other. It was the face of Craig Tyler, and Guy took a deep breath of satisfaction as he recognised his old enemy. *Now for it,* he thought. Any lingering doubts he might have had as to the identity of Peter Mersey's killer were wiped away by that one fleeting glimpse of that face; a face he knew so well from the past, and whose owner was a man of terror and ruthless action.

Guy was deeply puzzled, however, by the fact that the two arrivals made no attempt to move cautiously or search the cave in any way. In fact, they behaved as if the world of gloom in which they moved was entirely their own. Was it possible, then, that Tyler was unaware of Guy's presence after all? But the closed trapdoor — surely they must know.

And then, when Tyler himself spoke, Guy breathed freely again as the precious fact was borne in upon him that the two conspirators were indeed ignorant of their watchers.

'Hurry up, Mason. Remember that blasted trap closes after fifteen minutes.'

He looked at his watch. 'We've ten left to get the boat ready, bury the man, and clear out again. It means being stuck down here until the tide goes out if not.'

So the secret door was closed automatically! Nobody, then, had trapped them after all! Guy sighed with relief, but very soon his thoughts raised another problem in his mind. Even if Tyler was ignorant of the interest he and June were taking in his affairs, there was still nothing to account for the mysterious disappearance of the body from the cottage. Surely, thought Guy, the fact that he had left it covered with the tablecloth must have told his enemy quite clearly that someone else had found it, since no dead man could possibly shroud his own body. Puzzle as he would, Guy was unable to make head or tail of it. Tyler, who presumably had been instrumental in removing the corpse — even if he had not done so personally — must be aware that others now knew of the crime; yet his present behaviour certainly had none of the suspicions and caution Guy would have expected them to exhibit under the circumstances.

Troubled as he was by this fresh tangle with its as-yet unknown implications, he was given no time for further speculation, requiring his undivided attention with which to watch the movements of Tyler and Mason.

Together the two men walked towards the dinghy, the one addressed as Mason carrying a shovel, while Tyler shouldered a wooden box about three feet square. This he placed carefully on the ground against the cave side before turning to the boat.

'I thought you said he was dead when you put him here!' came the angry exclamation as Tyler saw that the body of Mersey was no longer in the boat but outside on the sand.

'He's dead enough now, anyway,' muttered his companion in a sulky voice, bending to examine him. 'Must've come round a bit and managed to get out — didn't get far though, so I don't see that it matters.'

Tyler grunted his disapproval. 'Well it's no use messing about; give me the shovel while you see to the boat. Sometimes I have grave doubts as to whether you're worth your keep, Mason. When I sent you up to bring that fool Compton down here, you put him right where I'd be most likely to fall over his useless carcass.'

Without waiting for any comment from Mason, Tyler began digging a hole in the sand, while Mason, grumbling to himself as he worked, turned the dinghy on its side and, making use of a jagged piece of rock for the purpose, stove in some of her planks just above the waterline. For a time Guy could make nothing of the reason for this, but then it dawned on him that after burying Mersey in the cave, the boat would be floated out at low tide to be found later on in a damaged condition with no one in it. It would then be assumed that the man who owned it had gone out sailing, struck some submerged wreckage or other obstacle along the neighbouring stretch of treacherous coast, and been drowned. When the tide went down far enough for the cave entrance to be navigable, they would take the dinghy out to the little harbour, step the mast, hoist a sail, and let it go free. A neat and cunning plot, thought Guy as he watched Tyler pull Mersey's shoes off and toss them to Mason, then carelessly dump the body into the freshly dug grave; the shoes, of course, as extra evidence to be found in the boat.

Guy tried to foresee the results of these activities. As soon as Mersey's disappearance was established as a case of loss at sea by accident, Tyler would be well placed to approach his victim's heir — who would presumably be June — and openly purchase Fortune Cay from her. Had it not been for the artist's letter to Sir Randolph bringing Guy onto the scene, it struck him as highly likely that Tyler's scheme would have borne fruit, for June would most probably have been perfectly willing to sell. Even if she had refused ... He shuddered at the consequences such an alternative woke in his imagination.

Tyler's position would have been stronger if he had not been compelled to shoot Mersey instead of drowning him, or killing him in some way which would have left his body usable as irrefutable evidence of death at sea. But for all that, Guy had a feeling that the man could have overcome the snags as successfully as he had done so many others.

What the poor woman's reactions must be as she watched from her vantage point the grim scene being enacted before her eyes on the beach, he tried not to think, for it must have been terribly hard on her after everything she had already endured.

Their gruesome task completed, Tyler and Mason — who from his appearance Guy guessed to be the second of Tyler's strong-arm men — straightened up; and, after a final glance round at the results of their handiwork, moved back to the stair, leaving no trace of the crime behind them.

While waiting for them to get far enough up the steps to be out of earshot, Guy was busy turning over in his mind the things he had seen and heard. His deductions were more sketchy than he could have desired, but Tyler's short speech during which he had upbraided his helpmate, Mason, has not only cleared Guy's mind on the subject of his enemy's apparent unconcern at the shrouding of the corpse in the cottage, but had also provided him with enough clues to fix a rough timetable of events and their sequence.

From what he had heard, Guy guessed enough to realise that 'Compton' must have been the name of the vanished body, and that Tyler in all probability had never seen the corpse covered by the tablecloth as Guy had left it. The most likely solution was that Tyler had sent Mason on ahead from Pardoner's Folly with the object of carrying both Mersey and the man Compton down to the sea cave, and that Mason, seeing the shrouded body of Compton, had probably been under the impression that Tyler had covered it. Mason's wits were obviously of doubtful brilliance, so that he had not been moved by sufficient curiosity to mention the matter to Tyler.

As far as Guy could see, it all fitted in. Mersey's capture and conveyance to Pardoner's Folly, the finding of June's telegram in his pocket, and the subsequent writing of the misleading note — all that must have taken place a short time before Guy's own arrival on the scene. Tyler would have sent one of his men to Fortune Cay to pin the false message on the door for any visitor, or for June herself to read.

Next came the departure of Elgin

Crossler, which Guy had witnessed with his own eyes. Then, during the time when he had been busy extricating June from beneath her car, Mersey had been taken to Fortune Cay, had his fight with Compton, succeeded in knifing him in the kitchen, and finally had been fatally wounded in the cellar.

Compton must have been left for dead on the kitchen floor when the others departed, possibly in a hurry for some reason or other; and later, between the time that June had fallen down the stairs and she and Guy had returned to the place for the second time, Mason had arrived and carried him down to the cavern, where, since he was no longer visible, he must already be buried.

So much Guy was able to deduce and reconstruct during the few moments of waiting. But, pleased as he was with the result, he still had very little to work on regarding the object of Tyler's ruthless determination to possess Fortune Cay and its convenient sea cave. Without more clues, he was stuck, but had high hopes that the wooden box Tyler had left would provide something fresh and enlightening to give him a lead.

He waited impatiently until the last glimmer of light finally disappeared and all sound of movement died away. Giving them a little longer for safety's sake, he stood erect in the chill water once more, stiff and very cold, looking upwards into the inky darkness. 'June,' he said quietly, 'are you all right?'

'Yes.' Her voice sounded shaky and stifled.

'Keep your chin up,' he said gently. 'I'm sorry I had to drag you into this.' He paused, then went on hurriedly in an attempt to divert her thoughts. 'You heard what Tyler said about the trapdoor closing. It's automatic. That's another piece of knowledge we've gained, and besides that we're now in a stronger position than before. While we know who Richmond is, he, on the other hand, is still ignorant of our existence.'

'Who is this man Tyler, Guy?' The faint inflection in her voice told him he had at least aroused her interest.

He sought to see in the darkness and

failed. 'A longtime and very dangerous enemy of mine.'

'And he — he — he killed ... Red?' The words quivered on her unseen lips, and instinctively Guy reached up in blackness. Their hands met and he took her slim fingers in a comforting grip.

'I'll make that an even score, I promise you,' he replied in an ominously quiet voice that boded no good for Tyler.

June was silent for a moment, and he was on the point of saying something else when she asked a question that caused him some embarrassment.

'Who and what are you, Guy?' Noticing his hesitation, she continued quickly: 'You're a strange man. Not once since I met you have I been able to make up my mind what was really happening. You seem to move in the dark as if the inside working of crime and wrongdoing was nothing new to you, yet you're not like a policeman, which I thought you might be at first.'

'I'm not a policeman,' he told her hastily. 'Put me down as just a public-spirited citizen. That's near enough for the purpose. I can't tell you any more than that, I'm afraid.

Maybe I'll be able to later on, but not now. Satisfied?'

'I suppose I'll have to be.' She sounded disappointed.

Guy was extremely anxious to examine whatever it was that Tyler had left behind. 'Hand me down the torch, will you? I'm going to have a look at that box, so stay here for the time being. I'll be back in a few minutes.'

She made no answer, but instantly the light came on and a moment later the flash-lamp was in his hand. He found on arrival beside it that the box was a stout affair, heavy and solidly made, while the lid was held firm by a neat lock. At first there seemed no way of opening it; but eventually, with the aid of his penknife, Guy managed to chip round the latch and raise the lid. Lifting an inner cover of waterproof plastic material, he sat back on his heels thoughtfully as he saw what lay exposed beneath.

Guy was no electrical engineer, but in his travels he had learnt to recognise all manner of strange things, and among them was the type of portable magnetic depth-recording instrument that was now before his eyes. In expert hands this small device, when carried over the surface of the water, could be read to show differences of level, however slight, on the sea bed below. In fact, with patience and skill, the shape of objects beneath the surface of the water over which it was passed could be recorded by means of a clearly readable graphical indicator drum mounted inside the machine.

Very ingenious and very useful, thought Guy; and, more important still, it provided him with a pointer to the course of Craig Tyler's activities.

8

Closing the lid of the recorder set, Guy scraped a hole in the sand and carefully buried the outfit, smoothing the surface and marking the spot with a stone. His discovery intrigued him, and though at first it was vague, an idea was gradually forming in his mind.

First there was Tyler's desire to obtain possession of the cottage and its cave. Then a boat called the *Arrow* came into the picture. If 'Pedro' — presumably in charge of the *Arrow* — was to bring it inside the cave, it must be quite a small vessel, and Guy would have given a lot to know its type and purpose.

And now there was the depth recorder. If that was intended for use on board the *Arrow*, it looked as if Tyler was engaged in something connected with the sea bed in the immediate vicinity of the coast, though what it might be Guy could not guess. One thing was clear, though: if Tyler was prepared to go to all this trouble — to say nothing of committing cold-blooded murder into the bargain — it must be of very high value to justify his actions.

Thinking on these lines, Guy came to the conclusion that until he actually saw the *Arrow* and found an opportunity to inspect it closely, he could make no further headway. Yet to remain in the cave until Tyler's next visit was inviting exposure, for as soon as the man missed the box, as he was bound to do the moment he looked for it, a thorough search would be made. But with the trapdoor closed above, and the cave mouth under water, how were he and June to effect an escape? For the life of him, Guy could see no way out.

He decided to let the problem rest, turning his attention instead to the damaged dinghy. Having already interfered with Tyler's plans to the extent of hiding the recorder set, he might as well go a step further and spoil his chances of using the boat for its intended purpose. If he put enough stones in it and allowed it to sink in the basin, its loss would give Tyler much food for thought; but before he did that, it seemed only logical to use the boat for reaching June in her hiding place. The splintered boards in the side would leak, of course, but at least it would save struggling along in the water as they had done before, and Guy was always a man to avoid discomfort if he possibly could.

Without more ado, he righted the dinghy and pushed it out onto the water. Shipping the oars, he sculled quickly towards the cleft in the wall, and then, standing up in the stern, told June to lower herself down.

It was the work of moments to regain the beach, and once there the two of them sat down side by side on the sand. Speaking in low tones, they discussed their situation, Guy explaining his ideas and telling her what he had found in the box. On the problem of escaping from the cave, however, neither had any useful suggestion to make, and it seemed as if they would have to wait until the entrance was clear at low tide.

'Pity we haven't got a couple of those frog-men outfits they used in the war,' Guy remarked with a rather bitter laugh, and he wondered why June made no comment as he had expected her to. When at last she did speak, her voice was earnest.

'I think we could do it without them, Guy.'

He turned his head in surprise. 'How?'

'By swimming underwater, of course.' Her enthusiasm increased as she enlarged on the idea. 'The arch that forms the entrance isn't very thick. It's just a case of locating it, diving under, and swimming. Let's try it — this place gets me down.'

He looked at her a little doubtfully. 'Can you swim well enough?' he asked, wondering what would happen if either of them misjudged it and struck the roof or sides of the narrow arch.

'Just try me!'

'Well, if you think you can manage it, I'm sure I can. But remember, we'll be doing it in pitch darkness, and it'll be risky.'

'More so than staying here?'

It was a challenge, and he saw the force of her words. 'No more, no less.' He rose to his feet. 'Where does the entrance lie?'

'I'll show you. Tell you what — we'll take the boat and dive from that.'

He smiled. 'You'd better stay in the

boat until I've had a feel round,' he countered. 'Then if it's feasible, we'll both go. Come on.'

With June sitting to one side of the dinghy so as to keep the splintered planks as much above the water as possible, Guy sculled towards a point on the blank wall of rock where she threw the beam of the torch. Swinging round opposite the spot she indicated, he lowered himself over the stern.

'How deep is it here?' he asked.

'About ten feet at high tide, I think.'

'Good. Shine the light downwards through the water, but for the love of Mike don't let it get wet. I won't be long.'

Taking in every cubic centimetre of air his lungs would hold, he ducked his head in a somersault dive and swam down until his fingers touched the sandy floor. The faintest green radiance from the light above showed the position of the dinghy, and, swimming to where he hoped the entrance was, he began exploring the wall with his hands. Just as his ears were beginning to sing, he felt the gap, and with a last effort groped further in to make sure. It was the entrance all right, and shooting to the surface, he found himself four or five yards from the boat.

'Over here, June,' he gasped.

When she pulled up to him, he hung on the stern for a moment, recovering his breath. 'You found it?' she asked excitedly.

'Yes. I'm going right through this time. Wait just here.' He paused, giving her the gun. 'If I don't return in under ten minutes, get back to the hole and sink the dinghy.'

She nodded. 'I'll be all right. But I won't stay here — I'll chance my luck and follow it … if you don't come back.'

For seconds he studied her face. This was no longer the woman who had knelt on the sand, crushed in spirit by her brother's death, but a wiser person, and one with plenty of nerve at that. She'd chance her luck all right; he knew that only too well. It suddenly became more important than ever to get through that black hole in the imprisoning walls of the gloomy cavern. For both of them.

Without another word he dived, this time entering the cave mouth with little difficulty. From then on, however, progress became one long, ghastly nightmare. Had there been daylight outside, or even a bright light inside, it would have been comparatively simple, but Guy had neither of these things to help him. In an ebony world of crushing water he felt his cautious way, his mind a prey to unanswerable questions and fears. How was he to know when to come up? How far could he go? Suppose he lost his sense of direction in this blind place — what then?

A rock grazed past his legs. Where the devil was he? For the first time he could remember, Guy was truly frightened. His chest was beginning to ache under the prolonged strain and his heart beat painfully. Desperately he moved onwards, though whether forwards or not he could no longer tell for sure. The keenest sight was worthless under such conditions, but a sudden twirl of movement flurried sand from the floor against his eyeballs, adding agony to fear. He blinked and made it worse; and then, when he felt he could last no more than a second longer, his way was barred. Barred by something huge that spread across his path.

A fearful mixture of panic and despair

seized him. This was the end. In a short moment his lungs must fill with the sandy saltwater. He wouldn't be able to prevent himself gasping it in, gulping hungrily for life-giving air — air that wouldn't be air at all, but water.

Too late to go back now. Mechanically, with the strength of a madman fighting for his life, he sought to thrust aside the thing before him; the thing that stood between himself and the outside world of freedom and air. Yes, air. He had to have that. Without it ...

His thoughts were blurring but he fought on, driven by panic, which in itself was a terrible thing. Under his frantic efforts the obstruction moved a little, swaying with dreadful slowness. The way ahead lay clear! He was free! Free to do what? Free to take that fatal gulp of air that wouldn't be air at all, but choking, suffocating water? No, not yet; please not yet. For a second? Two seconds? What was time? He gave heed only to the unbearable pressure in his chest. Time was bursting that as well. Time meant Death, with Peril laughing again beside him.

The salt was in his mouth; trickles of

it ran down his tightened throat. Up! He must get up!

Heedless of whether or not his head crashed against the roof, he kicked round the shifting obstacle and arched swiftly upwards. All he wanted to do was breathe. Nothing else. Water, or air, or sand; it didn't matter. Nothing mattered now; it was too late to live. His lungs were empty as the last of the stale air escaped through his nostrils. The salt in his throat became a flood; then suddenly it wasn't salt any more. He was coughing and choking, his mouth wide open.

With a splash that sounded like thunder in his ringing eardrums, his head came up, not to thud against unforgiving rock and be forced down again, but to feel the soft warmth of glorious air playing over his skin. Never in his life had Guy realised so fully the wonder of being able to breathe. In great gulps he sucked it in. It cleared his head, steadied the fearful pounding of his heart, and gave him back the power of coherent thought.

A few short strokes took him clear of the cave mouth, and, hoisting himself across a friendly hummock of rock, he thought back to those moments of terror in the entrance. Somewhat illogically, he found himself intensely interested in the nature of the thing that had barred his path and so nearly been the cause of his death. He remembered with a shudder how he had struggled to push it aside. Subconsciously his brain had registered its shape, but he was still so numbed by his experience that for a moment the memory of its form had no meaning beyond that of past fear. For a moment only; and then suddenly its significance dawned on him in an instantaneous blaze of staggering vividness. His brain grew icy cold.

He couldn't be wrong; there was no mistaking the feel of that hard sphere with its short, blunt protrusions. The stark realisation that down there in the cave mouth lay an unexploded mine set his nerves pricking. Drifting in on the tide, it must have somehow escaped going off on the rocks, and now rolled gently against the roof of the underwater entrance. *And Guy knew he must pass it again on his way back, or the woman inside would chance her luck.*

He put a hand to his head. The awful situation held no redeeming features in any direction as far as he could see. If June followed him, the odds were on her drowning, as he himself had so nearly done. Yet even if he did manage to make the return trip successfully, they would still be trapped, with enough high explosive to bring half the cavern down around their ears should it nudge against the rocks just a little too hard.

Yet what else could he do but go back? There was no other course open to him, for he realised more clearly than ever that during their adventures he had grown to think of June in a way that made her safety as important as his own.

Thrusting aside the dread he felt, he stood up on the slippery rock, braced himself for the effort, and dived once more into the danger-filled water.

His return to the inner cavern was less difficult than he had expected. The bulk of the mine confronted him sooner, of course, because it was nearer the seaward end of the tunnel, and pre-knowledge of what he must face gave him coolness of thought where before his mind had been ridden by panic. He was able to discover that between the mine and the wall of the cave was a narrow gap through which he could pass fairly easily. On the way out, the mine had been almost central, but the sluggish roll set up by his efforts had moved it to one side.

He eased himself through and swam on, an uncomfortable chill of fear running up and down his spine at the thought of the lurking power of destruction behind.

He bumped the rocky sides, fended himself off and pushed on, grim determination and the knowledge of danger adding whip to spur. The blackness pressed around him — close, unbroken, seemingly endless; and then at last came the faint gleam of the torch above his head.

With an enormous sense of relief he rose to the surface of the basin, and, gasping for breath, rested a moment or two, hanging from the stern of the dinghy.

June leaned over anxiously, her white face drawn into lines of worry, mingled with joy at the sight of his head. 'Oh Guy,' she said. 'I thought you were never coming. What's it like down there?'

'Hell!' he muttered thickly. 'There's an unexploded mine stuck halfway across. You'd never make it. We'll have to stay here until the tide goes out.'

She drew back, disappointment in her eyes. 'But if you went through and came back, there's no reason why I shouldn't. We can go together.'

She was going to be stubborn, he thought as he wearily pulled himself into the boat. He had no liking for the dilemma in which he found himself, but rather than lead her down into that devilish pit of peril and darkness to an almost certain death, he would stay in the cave, either until low tide gave them freedom, or Tyler's inevitable search forced a battle. So great had been the shock to his nerves when the mine had barred his way that he felt as if even gunplay with Tyler would be preferable to another trip through the entrance.

June, however, was adamant, and stood up, making the partially waterlogged boat rock dangerously by her sudden movement. Guy seized her wrist in a fierce, restraining grip. 'What d'you think you're going to do?' His words were firm.

118

'Dive!' she snapped, her eyes blazing. 'You've done it once, so it must be possible. If you're too scared to come with me, I'll go alone.'

Her voice was heavy with scorn, but though Guy resented it, he knew she failed to realise the danger. 'If I took you down there it'd be as good as murder. Please, my dear, don't be a fool. We're fine just here. I'm not afraid of Tyler, but I am afraid of losing you.' He stopped suddenly, realising the import of his words. Damn it all, he thought, he hadn't meant to bring sentiment into his arguments.

Still she stood above him, her eyes fixed on his dark face, her arm outstretched in the unrelaxed grip of his steely fingers. 'Are you?' She made no attempt to pull herself free, but there was a trace of wonder in her question, and something else besides; something Guy was unable to define.

He said nothing, but letting go his hold on her wrist reached out for the oars. 'Sit down,' he said. She did so, water slopping around her ankles in the bottom of the leaky boat.

Grimly he began to row towards their

hiding place. If they wasted much more time, he thought, the boat would sink under them. If they could reach the cleft in the rock, he could hold that against Tyler until they starved if need be.

Such was Guy's design. But, as so often happens, the obscure workings of Fate reverse the plans of men; and Peril, too, must have its fling.

With a sudden movement, June lunged out and grabbed Guy's arm with the strength of urgency. 'They're coming!' she gasped.

Twisting round, he saw again the light on the stairs that was the herald of danger. It danced brightly in the short interval of time before its bearer himself would make an appearance. The moment the man did, that there was no possible chance of reaching the hiding place before they were seen. Out there on the water they were fully exposed. Guy's hand was forced.

'Over the side,' he whispered in desperation. When June slipped quietly into the water he followed, taking the automatic from her hand as he did so. Hanging from the dinghy, he pushed the torch into his pocket and waited, a prey to expectancy.

With the boat forming a flimsy rampart between themselves and the beach, it would provide a little cover, and Guy was still reluctant to face the risks of the submerged passage until the last possible moment. 'Keep your head down,' he breathed.

'I'm going through the entrance now. Come with me. It's now or never — and I want to live.'

He found her arm in the darkness. 'Wait a bit. It's just possible that we might learn something before we go. There's far too much about this business that I don't understand.'

From the steps came a scraping noise, and the next moment the figure of Tyler showed up in the light of the torch he carried. He was alone, and over one arm was coiled what might have been an electric cable. Possibly something to do with the depth recorder, thought Guy. It was quite obvious, however, that if Tyler was on his own, they were unlikely to hear anything useful. It was, in fact, time to go before they were discovered.

'Hang on to this and don't let go, whatever happens,' he whispered in June's ear, pulling the tail of his shirt from inside his trousers as he spoke. 'He'll find the box and the dinghy missing in a moment. When I give the word, take a deep breath and hope.'

Before she could answer, there was a startled exclamation from Tyler, and Guy saw him searching round with frantic haste. It was as much as he could do to suppress a smile at the man's consternation; but when the light flickered across the water in a deep sweep and came to rest on the dinghy, his mouth set hard. 'Now,' he whispered, taking as deep a breath as possible.

Even as he spoke, the black world of the cavern was split by the flash of a gun and its echoing explosion. Again and again it came. One bullet whined away at a tangent from the rock wall to Guy's left; another splashed into the water in front of him with an angry hiss.

He heard June's steady intake of breath, paused just long enough for it to end, then dived. But before his head could dip below the surface his ears caught the sound of a gasp escaping her lips — a horrifying gasp that meant her lungs were no longer full; a gasp that might mean something worse.

9

The impetus of Guy's initial plunge carried them well down into the black depths, but he knew it would be fatal to attempt the passage of the entrance after hearing that ominous escape of breath. The only reason he could think of to account for it was that Fate had been unkind, and that one of Tyler's blind shots had found a billet in the woman. With a nameless dread in his heart, he swam upwards again. The fact that June still clung to his shirt gave him some little comfort, for had she been seriously injured he doubted if she would have been able to retain her hold.

The splash of their heads breaking surface brought a second fusillade of shots towards them, but all passed harmlessly overhead to strike the rocks above with splintering force. Guy slipped an arm round June and began swimming quietly through the water away from their present position. At that moment Tyler's flash-lamp went out as Guy sent a shot in the direction of the beam. All the time it remained out they were fairly safe, but if Tyler shone it again they would be at a serious disadvantage in their unprotected position in the water.

Guy put his lips close to June's ear. 'What happened?'

'Something hit me.'

'Think you can go on?'

He felt her nod her head vigorously in response. 'Yes, I'll make it. Just let me get my breath back.' Unpleasantly close, a bullet flicked past Guy's head, and waiting only for June to fill her lungs, he dived.

Prepared as he already was for what lay ahead, good fortune helped as well. Having played one dirty trick already, Fate relented, and more by luck than judgment they shot straight as an arrow into the hidden entrance. Even with the drag of June behind him, it was not many seconds before Guy's outstretched fingers rasped against the rusty metal of the mine. Shearing away a little, he felt round it, and was immensely relieved to find it still lodged to one side of the roof, leaving the gap open through which they could pass. Had it not been so, their plight would have been serious, for Guy was already practically at the end of his endurance.

Thankfully he came up, treading water, and slipped an arm round June's waist to support her weight. At long last they were out of the sea cave — but at what cost? Rapidly, he summed things up in his mind. The thing that troubled him most was the fact that June was wounded, though how badly he could not yet tell. A dreadful fear that it might be serious nagged at his imagination. Tyler, though temporarily at a disadvantage inside the cave, would hardly imagine his bullets had been lucky enough to kill them outright, and before long would realise the possibility of their escape by way of the entrance. The moment that dawned on him, a search would be made in the tiny harbour where they were now swimming, and from where Guy knew there was only one way out — up the steps cut in the cliff face to the cottage garden high above their heads. Out of the frying pan and into the fire, he thought grimly.

Floundering through the shallowing water, he scrambled to the dry, pebbly ground that served for a beach on one side of the inlet, pulling June as he went. Together they sank to the ground, he on his back, she on her face, both panting for breath and temporarily incapable of speech or anything else. Paramount in Guy's mind was the all-important question of whether or not June would be able to move far, for on that depended their next step.

As soon as he could speak, he asked: 'How badly are you hit?' It was impossible to keep the anxiety from his voice, and he made no attempt to conceal it.

'I don't think it's bad,' she answered, 'but it hurts.' She was still short of breath and sounded distressed.

He propped himself up on his elbow and looked down at her wet, bedraggled head. 'Whereabouts?' he asked gently.

For a moment she made no answer; then: 'It's my — the back of my leg, right — right at the ... top.' She faltered in some confusion.

'You mean you were hit in the backside,' he said somewhat unkindly, immediately guessing the reason for her hesitation. 'All right, my dear, it's nothing to be ashamed of. You couldn't help it, but it's a painful spot to catch a bullet I'm afraid.' He pulled the torch from his pocket, pessimistically pressing the switch, but, as he had half-expected, no helpful light rewarded him. The torch, then, was useless, owing to its immersion in the water, and was likely to remain so until it dried out. He thrust it back inside his pocket.

'Keep still and I'll see if I can find out how bad it is,' Guy told June. She raised no objection; but trying to examine a wound with only the faintest glimmer of starlight to see by, and uncertain even of its exact location, he discovered he was faced with quite a problem.

More by touch than any other sense, he found a long rent across the seat of her slacks; and then, to his great amazement, his gently probing fingers came up against something jaggedly sharp which seemed to protrude from the smooth, gleaming skin beneath. Puzzled, he gripped it between two fingers and gave it a tentative wriggle. June let out an 'Ouch!' and jerked violently, but by then Guy had guessed what had happened. One of Tyler's bullets, striking the cavern wall, must have sent a thin sliver of stone flashing down into the water to spear her when they were on the very point of diving. From the feel of it, Guy doubted it was embedded more than an inch or so in her flesh. If that was the extent of the damage, he thought with relief, the position wouldn't be so bad, since however painful the wound might be it was hardly likely to incapacitate her movements very much.

'I've found it,' he said. 'You've been harpooned like a whale! Stay quite still while I pull it out, and try not to yell.' At the same time as he spoke, he gave the splinter a sharp tug. It came out at an angle and must have hurt like the devil, but beyond a smothered yelp, June made no complaint.

'Wh — what was it?' she asked, rubbing her bottom tenderly.

'Lump of rock,' Guy answered laconically, handing it to her in the darkness. 'Maybe you'd like to keep it for a souvenir. How does it feel now?'

'Bit sore,' came the rueful reply. 'And the saltwater makes it sting. Is it — is it bleeding much?' She rolled over again.

'Not a lot,' he replied, 'but I can't very

well bind it up. Do you think you can walk all right? This isn't exactly a healthy place to hang around.'

She stood up experimentally, taking a few limping steps up and down the beach. 'I'll manage. But where are we going? There's no other way up from here apart from the cliff steps, and surely they'll be waiting for us at the top by the time we get there.'

The same thought had struck Guy just as forcibly. 'You're sure there's no other way up — further along the coast in either direction, for instance?'

June was silent for a moment, deep in thought. At last: 'There's a sort of fissure in the rocks about a quarter of a mile from here to the south. It is possible to climb it, but it's pretty tricky. I did it once with Red, but that was in broad daylight.'

'If we stay here Tyler will pick us off as soon as it's light. Besides, we've enough proof now to bring the police in and charge him with murder, so the sooner we clear out the better. Could you find this fissure in the dark?'

She hesitated for only a moment. 'Yes, I

think so, but with the tide in we'll have to swim most of the way.'

'Lucky it's calm then.'

Wasting no more time, they entered the water. June led the way with slow but steady strokes, and Guy, giving her all the time she needed, contented himself with following behind her on the landward side.

After going perhaps a hundred yards, she turned on her back and floated. 'Must have a rest — my leg's cramped.'

'No need to hurry,' Guy answered, coming up beside her. 'No sense in exhausting yourself — you'll need all your strength for the climb.'

He followed her example, rolling over and looking away into the darkness whence they had come. For several seconds he gazed back and up at the black-shadowed, barely visible cliffs. Against the velvet of star-dotted space, he could just make out the ragged skyline. Perched on it like a matchbox on a mantelshelf was Fortune Cay, home of an ill-fated man; home of Death, mysteriously mocking him with its secrecy, yet ever and anon teasing him with half-truths and glimpses of things when only the whole would suffice.

Guy wondered where it was going to end. He thought of the sea cave; the horror of those moments when the mine had almost trapped him; the whine of Tyler's bullets. What was the man engaged in? Clearly something to do with the sea, but what? If only he knew that!

But Guy did not know, and there lay the bare truth. He was little nearer solving the mystery than he had been when he drove away from Verity Hall with Sir Randolph's words echoing in his ears. And now it looked as if he never would know, for when they gained the cliff-top he would be bound to report what he had discovered to the police. Murder had been done, and there was no alternative — unless he took the law into his own hands and investigated Pardoner's Folly himself!

The idea grew in his mind; in fact it became more than an alternative, and showed itself to be the only logical course of action, because getting Tyler arrested for murder would still leave Elgin Crossler free to operate somewhere in the background. And with him around, whatever was afoot would remain so — even if the scene did shift to another setting.

Tyler would receive his reward for murder all right, of that Guy would make certain. And what matter if his inevitable end was postponed long enough for Guy to find out what was going on behind the veil in front of his eyes? As for June — eager as she was to avenge her brother's death, she would be more likely to fall in with the idea than raise any objection.

A splash from her informed Guy that she was once more swimming. Side by side this time, they proceeded for another few minutes before her wound forced her to call a second halt and rest.

'Sorry,' she said, 'but it feels as if a mule's kicked me.'

'I know just how you mean; some ill-mannered German once stuck me with a bayonet like that.' He could have told her the story, but said instead: 'Take it easy and I'll tow you in a minute.'

He rolled over. The sea was warm and delightfully restful to float on, and once again he puzzled in vain to unravel the tangle in his mind. A sea cave and secret stairway; the *Arrow* and its piratical-sounding Pedro; Elgin Crossler, Tyler, and a magnetic depth recorder. And something behind it all, like the picture on the lid of a jigsaw box, which made murder and risk and expense worthwhile to bring about an achievement — but what? Guy fervently hoped that entry to Pardoner's Folly would provide the answer.

He swam up in front of June, turned round, and, swimming on his back, slid his hands under her armpits to pull her along so that she need no longer use her legs. In this fashion they proceeded for some distance, until Guy was beginning to think they must be near the end of her quarter of a mile. Then with unexpected suddenness, a light appeared near the place where Fortune Cay stood foursquare to the sea. Below and above it, two smaller ones blinked into existence, so that to Guy, watching from the water, it looked remarkably like a signal set up for the purpose of guiding some boat in; though why the lights had not been placed at the bottom of the cliff to show the actual entrance of the inlet, he could not think.

Instinctively, while watching these

significant preparations, he stopped swimming, and the two of them remained for a space motionless in the gentle swell.

One thing was clear: if the lights were intended to guide the *Arrow* to Fortune Cay, the boat must be expected very shortly. It was a great temptation to Guy not to turn back and hide somewhere near the inlet in the hope of seeing it when it arrived. Had he been on his own, he would probably have done so, but in the circumstances the idea was impracticable.

As nothing further developed, he started swimming again, while June stared at the cliff for a sign of the place they sought. 'We're about there, I think,' she said presently. 'Mind the rocks — they're pretty bad round here.'

Her warning was fully justified, as Guy found to his cost during the next few minutes. Under shallow water were hidden sharp ridges, deep crevices, and dangerously smooth seaweed-covered edges. Slipping, sliding, and falling more than once, they picked their way through the deceptive shoals; and at last, grazed and bruised in a dozen places, they stumbled thankfully to the dark disorder of rocks at the base of the cliff.

'Now which way?' Guy asked, breathing hard.

'I'm not sure, but it isn't far from here, one way or the other.'

'We'd better split up, then. You go right and I'll go left. Try for a hundred yards or so, but if you don't have any luck in that direction come back here immediately and wait for me. Is there anything distinctive about this cleft?'

'Oh yes. You can't miss it once you're near enough to see it, because there's a high stone arch across the bottom.'

Guy was not really sure of the wisdom of splitting up in that way, but realised there was little immediate danger to be feared from Tyler, while on the other hand, saving time by searching separately would be a distinct advantage. He knew, too, that he would be able to move a lot faster than June; and, having covered the southern stretch, he fully expected to overtake her before she started back from the north to meet him. He watched for a moment as her small, limping figure disappeared in the darkness, then turned and made off in the opposite direction.

The going was rough and uneven. Most of the time he was clambering over rock falls or wading through pools waist deep. Once he floundered full length into an unseen crevice, skinning his leg and arm painfully. If he was having such a rough passage, he thought, how would June be faring under the same shocking conditions? He began to regret having sent her off on her own, and grew so anxious for her safety that he was on the point of retracing his steps, when ahead he made out the black outline of the high arch she had told him about.

Nearing it, he made his way cautiously round a tumbled mass of sea-smoothed boulders, and, peering up, tried to estimate the difficulties of climbing that would face them in their bid to reach the freedom of the open moor above. It would not be such a tricky ascent, he decided, if it was the same all the way up as the part he could see from where he stood.

Having reached this conclusion, Guy turned and began hurrying back in the direction he had come. He was just passing through the arch again when a sound came to his ears that caused him to pause and listen intently. Faintly at first, but growing louder every second, he heard the throb of what could only be a motor boat engine.

Standing back in the cover afforded by the arch, he waited, a little puzzled and vaguely worried. Since the moment they had seen the guiding lights set up at Fortune Cay, they had rounded a shoulder of the coast, and so, for some time now, had been out of sight of the cottage. The growing sound of the engine, then, could easily belong to the *Arrow*. But what worried Guy was the fact that it came not from the north, as if approaching the lights, but from the south, as if it had already passed them. That it could be any vessel other than the *Arrow* never entered his head, for he felt sure it was.

And then another, more uncomfortable, alternative presented itself. Suppose it was the *Arrow*, as he thought, not on its way *to* the inlet, but on its way *out* again, engaged in searching for the fugitives along the coast? Screened as they had been by the jutting shoulder of cliff, Guy had no means of telling whether at any time after they rounded it the boat had come up from the south, leaving them in ignorance of its arrival. If such was the case, its movements pointed directly to the fact that Tyler was now out in it looking for them.

Whether he knew of the existence of the fissure Guy had just located, he did not know, but it struck him that in the darkness the searchers would stand only a poor chance of seeing either himself or June if they kept quiet and lay hidden among the scattered rocks. There was such ample cover on that part of the coast that he was confident they would be able to elude discovery.

A moment later, however, when he judged the invisible boat must be level with him and about eighty yards from the shore, he had cause to think again. Without warning, the blazing beam of a small but powerful searchlight shot out from the vessel; and as it moved slowly across the rocks, Guy felt he must be seen for certain in the brilliant glare.

Instinctively he crouched down in the shelter of the arch, and for long seconds held his breath as the light raked among the shadows behind him, searching the full extent of the fissure above. This action removed any doubt that the boat was anything but the *Arrow;* and, in spite of the imminent risk of discovery he was in, Guy felt relieved to realise that, had it not been for the delay caused by June's wound, they would probably have been halfway up that naked place by now, presenting a perfect target for the slowly cruising boat. Silently he blessed the small sliver of stone that in the long run had undoubtedly proved their salvation.

Finding no sign of them, the revealing pencil of light swung away; and, coming from his hiding place, Guy set off as fast as he could in its wake, hoping meanwhile that June would guess what this fresh danger was and find cover before they had a chance of seeing her. That stabbing beam gave Guy the same feeling as he imagined an animal might have when it was being hunted. He cursed himself again for not keeping June beside him instead of separating. Not that there was much danger of her being seen, for she had enough good sense to keep out of sight; but it would have been comforting if he could have made certain of the fact.

Hastening with all speed, Guy heaved a sigh of relief when the searchlight suddenly flicked out and darkness came down once more in a blank, oppressive wall. The muffled throb of the boat's engine as it cruised slowly along the coast was still audible, but he decided its occupants had probably given up the search, realising the insurmountable difficulties of finding anyone on such a rugged beach.

So much the better. There were enough risks to contend with as it was, and the thought that they would now have to climb the fissure with the added danger of a floating searchlight which might at any time find them was disturbing, to say the least.

Another thing that was beginning to worry Guy was the time factor. He had no idea what time it was, for his watch had stopped long ago, and so much had already happened that it might be any hour for all he knew. The darkness was now of that black intensity that comes before the dawn, and to be caught still at the base of the cliff when daylight came would be disastrous.

Spurred to even greater efforts by this fresh thought, he hurried on, for to find June and lead her back to the cleft was now of the utmost urgency if they were to succeed in making good their escape.

Reaching and passing the place where they had separated, Guy peered keenly ahead for any sign of her, and it was then that he heard the engine of the *Arrow* returning. His heart beat faster at the sound. Was it worth risking a call? The noise of the boat's motor and its progress through the water would drown it, he decided, and he badly wanted to know where June was, for by now he ought to be somewhere near her.

'June,' he called softly, not daring to raise his voice very high.

'I'm here.' Her words came faintly from some distance away.

'Coming,' he answered with some relief, and he made off in the direction of her low cry as fast as he could.

The sound of the boat was close now, and, coming to a halt, he realised it would be wise to take cover until it passed. Lowering himself into a nearby pool so as to be out of sight, he waited.

For a few moments he crouched down tensely, up to his neck in the water, and then the thing he was afraid of happened. Once again the white finger of light groped out from the sea, tearing away the darkness at the base of the cliff, and suddenly becoming motionless as it held a spot among the rocks in vivid relief.

In the very centre of the patch of brightness was the prone figure of June, where, by sheer bad luck, the beam had caught her several yards from cover of any kind.

10

With a sinking heart, Guy realised the boat was creeping inshore towards the rocks and pools that fringed the cliff base. June lay on an isolated patch of sand, and it was sickening to think that had the light delayed for ten seconds longer, she could easily have reached the shelter so amply provided by the nearest pile of boulders.

Her position was perhaps fifty yards north of where he himself now lay in hiding, and the *Arrow*, working its cautious way in, was roughly the same distance away, so that the three formed a triangle which, as the boat came in, was continually changing shape.

Guy watched helplessly, his brain racing in an endeavour to find some way out of the mess. It would be impossible for him to reach the woman without being seen, while to remain where he was would give him some advantage over the party in the boat; but in the meantime, Tyler, he knew, was perfectly capable of shooting her down in cold blood.

With that all-revealing light pinning her down, she would never be able to gain cover before being picked off by the boat, and Guy suffered a nasty moment of fear when he saw her rise to her feet and begin to run like a frightened rabbit. Hardly had she moved, however, before the sharp crack of a rifle rang out and an angry spurt of sand kicked up in front of her. Instantly realising the danger, June immediately stopped, then raised her hands in token of surrender.

Surely, thought Guy in a fever of dread, she did not for one moment imagine that Tyler would honour such a gesture! With an uncontrollable shudder he pictured the man in his mind as he calmly drew a bead on her heart and gently squeezed the trigger. At any moment now the fatal report would come.

Without hesitation, regardless of the fact that his action would give away his own position, Guy shouted desperately to her to lie down. Even as he saw her give a start at his cry and fall to her face, the crack of the rifle came again, but the eerie *wheee* of the bullet ricocheting harmlessly away off the rocks told him that mercifully she was still unhurt.

The grace his timely warning had given her could only last for seconds, however; for, exposed as she was, her body must still present a good enough target for any average marksman — and Tyler, he had cause to know, was above average. There was only one thing to do if Guy was to provide her with another chance.

Dragging his automatic from his pocket, he raised himself and sent a shot crashing towards the boat. The range, he knew, was too great to register a hit except by a lucky fluke, but the report alone had the desired effect, for next instant the beam of the searchlight swung away from June and concentrated on sweeping the general area from which his shot had come.

Ducking down out of sight again, he waited breathlessly. For an endless time, the light poked about, sometimes above his head, at others to left or right, but never very far off and often uncomfortably close. Once when it looked as if it would return to where he had last seen June, he fired again, and was rewarded this time by an angry shout from the *Arrow*.

In spite of the success he had so far achieved in distracting attention from June to himself, Guy knew their position was little better than it had been before. Any movement he made beyond his present cover would quickly be seen in the glare, yet if he was pinned down for much longer the chances of escaping from the cliff base before dawn would be remote; and after that, neither he nor June would stand much chance of survival, for his automatic was but poor protection against rifle fire. If only there was some way of putting the searchlight out of action! Unless he could succeed in doing that, Guy might as well count this his last adventure, and he had no intention of doing that while he still had life in his limbs.

Seizing a moment when the probing light was hovering some distance away, he pulled himself clear of the pool, and, darting forward, lessened the distance between himself and the boat by several yards. It was already considerably nearer than it had been earlier, for after his first distracting shot Tyler had edged further south, so that now not more than twenty-five yards separated them.

Guy's whole plan depended on being able to get near enough for an accurate shot at the searchlight, but how exactly he was to do it he failed to see, since the closer he approached the more readily visible his movements would be in the local diffusion of the concentrated beam. He chanced another slithering advance under cover of a short range of rocks — and then, at last, fortune smiled on his efforts. From where he now lay, to the almost stationary boat was open water.

Gathering all his strength, and bunching his muscles tensely for the coming ordeal, he raised himself to his hands and knees. With a sudden shout from the *Arrow* echoing in his ears, he plunged into the water, and, a moment later, was swimming beneath the surface towards the brilliant radiance that marked the boat's position.

With a pounding heart, Guy came up close alongside the boat under the very noses of the enemy. Shaking the water from his eyes, he looked upwards. Clearly silhouetted against the dipped beam of the light was a profile he recognised as Tyler's, while beside him was that of another man. Both held rifles poised ready as they peered down into the depths from which they expected him to rise, and dearly would he have loved to have sent his bullets not at the light, but at the two heads peeping eagerly over the side. The target they presented, however, was too small to risk the hard-earned chance he had gained; while, on the other hand, obliterating the searchlight was comparatively simple now that he was close. Praying silently for the few precious moments he needed, Guy raised his gun and pressed the trigger.

Instantaneously, pandemonium broke loose. Both men in the boat fired wildly as Guy emptied the magazine of his gun coolly and deliberately into the white-hot centre of the searchlight. When suddenly it dimmed, flickered for an instant, then vanished with a faint hiss, he took a deep breath of satisfaction. Now, he thought, life would be very much simpler.

With the extinguishing of the light, Guy's hopes rose by leaps and bounds. Having run appalling risks in carrying out his sortie, he now sank swiftly beneath the wavelets, swam underwater for a safe distance, then came up again, the old sardonic smile playing round the corners of his mouth.

After the vivid glare of the light, he found himself almost blind in the ensuing darkness, but had already seen enough of the *Arrow* to recognise it for what it was — a low-built, powerful motor launch. What intrigued him far more than that, however, was the gaunt outline of a stubby crane or derrick, complete with block and tackle, that appeared to be built out over the stern. The sight of this and the inferences he drew from it gave him much food for thought; and, feeling well satisfied with his efforts, Guy went down again and made for the rocks.

Scrambling ashore, he hurried towards the place June had last been visible, veering south as he went in the direction of the fissure, for he felt sure that once free of the light she would have made for that.

To put as much distance between themselves and the boat before pursuit began was imperative; but, before he could think of starting, he must find June. Then, together, they could gain the cliff top. The whole plan, he knew, depended for its success on speed, and in consequence he redoubled his efforts.

Behind him he could hear voices, followed a moment later by a scraping noise as the boat ran in alongside the rocks. Grimly it came to him that he was not going to have it all his own way after all. A glance over his shoulder revealed the light of a flash-lamp wavering about as someone, presumably Tyler, leapt ashore and began to hunt among the rocks and pools in a gradually widening arc. By now, however, Guy was well over halfway to the base of the cliff, travelling with desperate haste and confident of evading capture. Indeed, so high were his spirits that he became far more intent on locating June than worrying about Tyler. Where she had moved to when the light swung away, he could only guess, and he was beginning to wonder how on earth he should find her, when suddenly to his dismay his feet slipped from under him on a seaweed-covered ledge, and with a splash that must have been audible on the *Arrow*, he went down full length in a shallow pool.

Letting out a savage oath, Guy scrambled up, realising the noise would certainly have given him away to his pursuers. Almost immediately his fears were confirmed by a shout from Tyler to the other man who had joined him. A blind shot whined overhead, followed by the noises of their hurried progress growing nearer.

Guy stumbled on, fearful lest the beam of the torch picked him out; and then, when he was nearly frantic with worry at not finding June and half-exhausted from his desperate haste, he caught the sound of his own name being called very softly from a dark mass of rocks close by on his left. Thankfully he darted towards it, his hopes rising again when a moment later he made out a small patch of lighter tone where June's face gleamed faintly from the shelter of a deep, waterlogged rift.

Sliding in beside her without a word, he crouched down, swiftly pressing a fresh clip of cartridges into the empty magazine of his gun. Although Tyler was as yet uncertain of their exact position, he and his companions were widening their search and drawing closer every second. Unless the two fugitives could slip away, the game was up; for if they stayed where they were, it would mean a pitched battle with all the advantages on the side of the enemy.

Guy could, of course, wait and ambush Tyler and his fellow searcher when they approached near enough, but decided the risks involved in such a plan were too great to take. It would only need a flash from the torch in his eyes to dazzle him so effectively that accurate shooting would be out of the question. Within minutes their hunters would easily pick them off from a safe distance, or alternatively, simply sit down and wait until daylight made it impossible for them to escape.

No, he decided, this was an occasion when flight offered the best possibilities. Whispering to June to keep silent, he stood up, and, groping round in the dark, felt for a loose stone. Having secured a suitable one for his purpose, he hurled it with all his might in a direction which, if he heard the sound of its fall, would lead Tyler on a wild goose chase away from them.

June crawled up beside him, and, when the clatter of the stone falling among the rocks caused their pursuers to hurry towards the source of the disturbance, he grabbed her by the arm and urged her over the scattered boulders in pursuit of the fissure that was their only hope of escape. In view of her wound and the numerous minor cuts and bruises that had been added to it since they left the sea, she made remarkably good time over the shockingly rough ground, so that Guy had no need to impress on her the absolute necessity for speed.

All sounds of pursuit had now faded away in the distance. The success of his ruse had been complete, and he felt confident that if they could once gain the fissure, most of their troubles would lie behind them. Breathlessly they stumbled on, anxiously peering ahead for the high stone arch that marked their goal; and when at last it loomed up in front of them, Guy led June into the shelter of the cleft with a sigh of relief. Both of them flopped weakly against the rocks, and Guy, recovering quickly, realised that June was badly spent after their mad career along the shore. He was compelled to wait until she was fit enough to attempt the climb.

It was, in fact, fully five minutes before she announced herself capable of going on; and then began an ascent which in later years was to rank among Guy's memories as one of the most unpleasant half-hours of his life. Probably, he thought, it might have been reasonably easy to scale the tortuous scar in the cliff face by the full light of day; but now, unable to see in the darkness further than a few feet above his head to the next handhold, climbing became a nightmare — a fearful dream fraught with danger at every move, with horrible death on the rocks below for the one who slipped or missed their footing.

More than once as they struggled upwards, Guy had cause to thank his lucky stars for having taken the precaution of roping June to his waist. By means of his shirt, her own woollen sweater and a cardigan she had been wearing, he had linked the two of them together; and, though the safety of such a rope was doubtful, it did give her some assistance, besides having a helpful effect on their nerves.

155

The fissure, he found, was not the same all the way up as he had hoped it would be after his first hasty survey. Instead the going deteriorated some twenty feet from the bottom, so that several times their position was precarious in the extreme. On one occasion June slipped backwards a matter of six inches, and only by a superhuman effort was Guy able to retain his hold and at the same time grab her to prevent her falling. The experience shook them both considerably, and woke in Guy's imagination a vivid idea of what could so easily happen through the slightest error of judgment.

Working as near blind as made no matter, they clambered on, badly frightened and rapidly growing tired from the exertion. Guy, experienced climber as he was, found himself hating every inch of the awful journey, and it was only the thought of what lay below on the beach that forced him ever upwards, spurring him in desperation to reach the wild freedom of the moor that was their ultimate goal.

Every foot they gained was in itself a major victory, and slowly but surely they mounted higher in the velvet darkness, straddling the narrow cleft, until finally, just below the cliff top itself, there came a place where a fallen boulder had jammed solidly across it, apparently closing off all hope of further advance.

Guy looked up in dismay, fearful that now, after getting so far, Fate was going to take a cruel delight in laughing in their faces at this, the eleventh hour. Desperately he strained his eyes in the darkness for cracks or projections that would serve as holds to work round the obstruction. Near the outer edge of one of the side walls of the fissure was a single, scanty hold roughly at shoulder level, but at least a foot beyond his reach; and, search as he would, Guy could see nothing else by which to gain it. Below, but further out still, was a suitable footing from which to work; and, once there it would be possible, though extremely hazardous, to climb round the huge lump of rock that barred their way.

The seemingly insuperable difficulty that confronted them, however, was to bridge those few feet to the all-important holds. For a time it seemed as if they would be forced to abandon any hope of reaching the safety that lay so tantalisingly close beyond the cliff top; and then, when he was on the point of telling June his fears, Guy thought he saw a way out. But it meant they would have to proceed one at a time, and one at a time meant untying the rope.

Much as he dreaded the idea of severing that precious though flimsy lifeline, it was either that or stay where they were, for to descend would be courting death at Tyler's hand. So, explaining the position to June, Guy undid the rope from around her waist, telling her to wedge herself firmly into the cleft. Then, using her hands to take part of his weight, he swung himself up and out to reach the little projection. If his fingers or his feet missed their aim, he knew he must go crashing down to the shore below; but with his life depending on it, he made no mistake. Moments later he was beginning to crawl like a fly past the obstructing piece of rock.

Without the extra spring of the lift he obtained from June, the manoeuvre would have been completely impossible; but as it was, success rewarded him. Perspiration streamed down his forehead and ran into his eyes as he edged his way inch by inch to the comparative safety of the upper face of the boulder. When he finally gained it, panting and spent, a fearful reaction swept over him. His muscles grew suddenly weak; for a moment even his brain refused to function. It was only by an enormous effort of willpower that he gathered his wits together and established himself securely in preparation for the next step — a step he was terrified to take, yet knew he must: that of getting June to safety beside him.

His idea — the only feasible one to complete the plan he had in mind — was to lower the rope down from where he was so that she could swing out on it across those few impossible feet and climb the rest of the way as he himself had just done. The danger came, he realised with cold fear in his heart, during that split second of swing, for then her whole weight would depend on the doubtful strength of their rope.

Would it not be better to wait for morning, rather than risk her life so lightly? Even now, though he knew he was already committed, Guy hesitated. The memory of Tyler's sharp-shooting, however, decided him; there could be no turning back from his resolve, and at least they had a fair chance this way, whereas the other alternative could only end in certain death.

With his feet set tightly against the fissure wall, Guy lay down and loosened the rope from his waist. Then, stretching out as far as he could, he let the end dangle into space. 'Can you reach it?' he called softly.

'Not by a good six inches,' came her disappointed reply.

'Hang on then. I'll have to lengthen it by adding my trousers.' Quickly he wriggled out of his corduroys, lashed them firmly to the end of the rope, then tried again. 'Tie it under your armpits,' he said.

He felt her pulling gently as if adjusting it, then: 'All right,' she called. 'Say when — I'm ready.'

Guy tightened his grip and braced himself, his nerves tingling madly as he thought of the peril June must face. Everything now rested on the rope; the doubts in his mind shouted to him to stop before it was too late, but he refused to heed them. 'Try not to jerk,' he said, thrusting away the insistent clamour of his fears. He wanted to sound calm, but fear in itself made his voice unnaturally harsh. 'Let it take the weight steadily if you can — and don't be scared.'

He felt a stretching as her woollen sweater gradually gave; and then, when he knew she must be putting the full strain on it, he felt her swing. Like the shaft of a pendulum, the frail line moved to one side. His ears caught the sound of a frightened gasp; a scraping noise on the rock face; the sound of a loosened pebble falling ... falling ... falling.

If only it wasn't so dark! He eased himself over a little. With horrible clarity he could picture June hanging beneath him over the awful void. Would she never get a footing? The rope gave the tiniest jerk and seemed to jump in his fingers. Surely it was breaking! Oh God!

In a fever of suspense he waited; whether for half a second or twenty he never knew. And then the strain on his arms eased slightly. Never had he been so glad of anything in his life before, for it could only mean that her feet had found a purchase. The sweat was pouring off him; the palms of his hands were wet and slippery.

'Guy.' Her voice was shaky. 'Don't pull too hard — I think your shirt's beginning to tear.'

The words brought his heart leaping to his throat in a fresh wave of terror. 'Are you all right?' he managed to ask.

'Yes — so far; I've got my feet on the ledge but I can't find a handhold.'

'It's level with your head and a little to the right. Got it?'

He held his breath. Suppose she was unable to reach it? Every muscle in his body cried out for rest. Wracked with fear and exhaustion, he hung on to the strand that held June back from the arms of Death.

Suddenly he heard her voice again, steadier this time: 'I've found it!'

Presently, as he himself had done, she started climbing. He dare not give her more than the barest support with the rope, for fear it would rip apart and send her crashing down to the rocks below. His pulse was like a clock — every beat a thousand years; and with every beat fear gripped his heart more closely.

If she slipped so much as an inch! It would be nothing less than murder. Murder of someone brave and stout-hearted; someone who grew more and more important to him as time dragged its leaden feet. Guy shuddered in the self-imposed torture of his vivid imagination.

And then, at long last, her small, bruised fingers came creeping over the edge. Letting go of the rope, he seized her wrists with fierce exultation, pulling her bodily up beside him with a final heave. His weariness and exhaustion temporally forgotten, he clasped her limp body tightly in his arms, rocking her to and fro as if she were a child. Conscious only of how unutterably thankful he was to have her safe with the worst part of their ordeal behind them, Guy gave no thought to anything else.

She was shaking like a leaf, the very fibres of her young being torn by reaction and horror, but after a few minutes she recovered sufficiently to show her eagerness to finish the climb. Guy, too, recalled his mind to the task in hand. They might have overcome the worst part, but were not, he knew, out of the woods by any means.

There was now not more than six or seven feet of the crevice above their heads.

Beyond the jagged skyline would lie the moor, and — Pardoner's Folly.

Swiftly he led the way up the final stretch. It was easy compared with what had gone before, and, hauling himself over the rough edge, he turned and pulled June to his side. Almost completely done, they both sank in a panting heap on the ground, grateful to feel solid earth once more beneath them.

Guy closed his eyes, telling himself again and again that the peril to which he had so recently exposed June had been fully justified. He wondered if she realised what a near thing it had been. She lay beside him, silent except for the rhythm of her gulping breath, thankful for life, but still a little frightened. Guy opened his eyes and looked at her. In that moment he knew just how closely their lives had come together during the last hours of night. Did she feel it too? Did she ...

'Put yer 'ands up and don't move!'

The rasping command came simultaneously with the light of a powerful torch that leapt from the darkness to hold them in its beam.

Guy froze rigid at the utter unexpectedness of the harsh words, at the same instant remembering with a sudden sense of helpless fury that his gun was in the pocket of his corduroys — and his corduroys still dangled loosely in June's hand, a part of their rope.

Slowly he raised his arms in mute surrender.

11

Baffled, enraged by his own carelessness, and blaming himself a dozen times over for being such an imbecile as to forget his weapon, Guy waited while whoever was behind the torch stepped forward. As the man moved, a little light spilled for a second on the revolver that was levelled so uncompromisingly at them.

Dazzled by the beam as it came back full in his face, Guy wondered who this might be. Often enough he had smiled at the saying 'caught with his trousers off', but to be in that unenviable position himself was ironic and not very funny.

Had he had the slightest sense he would have remembered the gun in his pocket before making his trousers part of the rope, but so anxious had he been to get June to safety that no thought of it had entered his head. Guy put a black mark against himself, hoping meanwhile that he would live long enough to redeem the result of his gross mistake.

His self-condemnation occupied no more than seconds, and by then their captor had advanced and now stood a few yards away. Coming to a halt, he spoke for the second time: 'Where's your gun? I know you've got one 'cause I 'eard it.'

'I always wear it next to my skin!' was Guy's purposely facetious reply. Considering that he now wore nothing but a vest and underpants, the man would hardly expect to find it on his person, and he knew the chances of getting the weapon from his trouser pocket before being shot down were too thin to risk.

With something like a snarl the man came nearer, and Guy recognised him as Mason. The one who had been with Tyler on the beach, then, must have been Pedro, he thought.

'It's no good actin' funny, mister, 'cause I know all about you. Come on, now — where's that gun?'

'Find it!' snapped Guy, but hardly had he spoken before June cut in.

'Don't argue with him!' she cried. Then,

to Mason: 'It's in these trousers tied to the other things — here.' She tossed the rope across to him so that it fell a little short.

Now, wondered Guy, what the devil was she playing at? A moment later he realised, for as Mason stooped warily to draw the clothes towards him, he was forced to use the hand in which he held the torch. For an instant the light was deflected off them, and in the small relaxation Guy saw his chance and seized it.

Twisting rapidly to one side, he threw himself into the shadows beyond the light, rolled into the bracken, and scrambled away. If he could only draw Mason, June might retrieve his trousers and so regain the precious automatic.

The beam of the torch followed his flying figure. Two shots rang out, one bullet spattering Guy's face with dirt as it struck the ground. He heard a curse and lumbering footsteps behind; and then, catching his foot in some trailing undergrowth, he went down heavily.

Winded by his fall, and still only partially recovered from the climb up the fissure, Guy attempted to rise; but before he even got to his knees, Mason was on him. In the wavering light of the torch, he saw with a sinking heart that the man still grasped the rope of clothing. His bid had failed!

It was a bitter disappointment, but determined to sell his life dearly, he came up fighting, launching himself at Mason before he had time to level his revolver. His opponent, however, was too quick for him. As Guy tried to grapple and force him into a clinch, Mason lifted his foot and kicked him full in the stomach. Staggering backwards into the gorse, Guy crumpled up, blinded by pain and speared in a thousand places by the vicious spines.

Mason laughed brutally at his discomfort, and, drawing back his foot, caught him again with his heavy boot before directing the beam of the torch on his face. 'Just for that,' he rasped, 'I'm goin' to kill you now and save meself trouble — Mister Richmond won't mind!'

He raised his gun slowly, taking his time and watching Guy's twisted face. Gasping for breath, his stomach one great area of acute agony, Guy closed his eyes. Nice way to finish, he thought, just as everything looked as if it might work out. With a sickening dread, he wondered what would happen to June. At least it would be some consolation if she had managed to make her getaway in the commotion. He looked at Mason again. The man was a mountainous shadow towering above him.

What was he waiting for? The shape of the revolver steadied, the black muzzle pointing straight between his eyes. Guy clenched his fists and dropped his eyelids again just as the roar of the explosion beat against his eardrums. He felt deafened; conscious of nothing; no tearing pain as he expected. This wasn't so bad. Quick and painless! Often enough he had wondered what it would be like to die. He could still see Mason, too; that was funny. And then suddenly the man seemed to rear up, crumple at the knees, and, a moment later, was falling down on top of him in an obliterating avalanche of crushing weight.

'Guy! Guy!' The wavering voice was June's. He shook his head in a daze of bewilderment. Almost immediately she was kneeling beside him, frantically tugging and heaving at Mason's limp body. A few seconds afterwards, when Guy, still uncertain whether he was alive or dead, struggled out from underneath, she sat back on her heels with something halfway between a sob and a sigh. In her hand was his own automatic, thin wisps of acrid smoke still crawling lazily from its muzzle.

'How the devil ...' he began in amazement, looking from her gun to his clothes where they lay beside Mason.

June smiled weakly. 'Oh, that,' she said. 'I had it in my slacks all the time. When you threw the rope down for the second time, I felt it in your pocket and took it out. I forgot to tell you about it before.'

'Lucky for me you did.' He paused. 'You're quite a woman, aren't you, June? You know you saved my life just then? I don't know how —'

'Please, Guy, let's go,' she interrupted hurriedly, jumping to her feet.

He scrambled up, then bending over Mason made a rapid examination of the man. He was quite dead, June's bullet having taken him full in the centre of the back. 'Nice shooting.' It was a warmly appreciative comment.

'Oh!' She sounded a little frightened. 'You mean I killed him?'

Guy grinned. 'Very much so, my dear — thank you.'

'What should we do now?'

'First of all,' he answered, 'we'll push the body out of sight. Then I'm going to get dressed, after which we'll retire gracefully from the morbid battlefield.' So saying, he took the revolver from Mason's fingers, handed the flash-lamp to June, and rolled the bulky form of the dead man under the gorse bush that had so recently been his own uncomfortable bed. June, meanwhile, had untied their clothes, put on her sweater and cardigan, and now stood waiting with his shirt and trousers ready.

Guy's back still smarted from the myriad punctures it had suffered when Mason kicked him into the bush; but, though his stomach ached horribly from the vicious impact of the man's boot, he found himself apparently unhurt in any other way. Hastily pulling on his clothes, he led June inland, heading in a direction he thought would bring them out on the track across the moor. Tyler and his companion must have heard the shots fired by June and Mason, he realised, and before long would come streaking back to Fortune Cay with the intention of finding out the reason — or the result — of the shooting.

Guy's plan now was to do as he had intended once before: leave June hidden safely in the Bentley where it was concealed in the hollow just off the track, and then, taking advantage of the last of the dark hours, gain entry to Pardoner's Folly in order to probe the mystery of Tyler's activities from that end.

They spoke little as they hurried over the rough moorland, Guy busy with his own perplexing thoughts, and June, he knew, silent in her uncomfortable efforts not to slow the pace on account of her limping. He guessed, too, that she was somewhat shaken by the fact that she had recently killed a man. It was a good thing, he decided, that her scruples had not asserted themselves at the time, or he would have been dead. His already high estimate of her worth went up considerably.

Then he began wondering about Tyler. His enemy must be getting short-handed by now. Peter Mersey had said in his letter to Sir Randolph that 'Richmond' had two men, one a deaf-mute. Thinking back to the dying man on the cottage floor, Guy remembered that he had made no sound whatever during the short time he had seen him alive. It seemed certain, then, that he had been the deaf-mute Compton. With Mason dead as well, Tyler's forces could consist only of Pedro, for Guy was sure there had been no one else aboard the *Arrow*. There was, of course, always Elgin Crossler to be counted in the team, but Guy had seen him leave in something of a hurry. So much the better. The odds against them were quite fearful enough as it was.

He brooded for some time over the inference to be drawn from what little he had seen of the *Arrow*. The short, stout crane rising over its stern, coupled with his discovery of the depth recorder outfit, pointed unmistakably to submarine work of some kind. Was Tyler looking for something on the sea bed, using the sea cave as a base to work from? It was certainly the only solution he could think of, and, as far as he could decide from the facts in his possession, the only one that fitted the bill. It must be salvage work of some kind.

He toyed with the idea for a few moments. It was undoubtedly a reasonable guess, yet it was unlikely to be anything in the nature of heavy work, since the available equipment of the *Arrow* would hardly be capable of raising a sunken rowboat, let alone anything of the size worth the desperate measures Tyler had already taken to preserve his secret. Unless it was something small, and at the same time of great value. Such as — what?

Guy puzzled on and on in this way until they reached the track and struck off along it in the direction of the Bentley. He had already outlined his plan roughly for June, but when they arrived at the car she showed a strong inclination to argue, protesting against being left on her own when she might be of use to him elsewhere. He flatly refused to consider her suggestion that she should go with him to Pardoner's Folly, pointing out that the chances of his gaining useful information would be more than doubled if he was free to work alone. Quite apart from that, he had no intention of exposing her to any further danger if it could possibly be avoided.

She seemed a little puzzled at his obvious determination to follow up the events that had gone before. 'Why can't we go straight to the police, Guy? Surely you've already done more than any public-spirited citizen could be expected to do in the circumstances?'

For a moment he was silent, peering at her closely in the gradually lightening darkness; then: 'I'm not just 'any public-spirited citizen', June,' he murmured.

She frowned slightly, digesting his remarks. At last: 'You mean you're a detective?'

'Put it that way if you like,' he said with a faint grin.

'Oh!' For some reason or other that he could not fathom, she sounded disappointed. 'I thought ...'

'Listen,' he interrupted earnestly, 'I promise you this — your brother's murderer shall not go free. But so much else comes into the picture besides his death that I must ask you to leave things entirely in my hands. I have my own way of carrying this party to what I hope will be a successful conclusion.' He paused, going on in a softer tone: 'Your brother was an unfortunate pawn in the game, no more. I'm sorry, but that's the cut of it. Now what do you say?'

He was totally unprepared for the result of his speech. 'What's to stop me going to the police on my own as soon as you've left me here? I don't understand what it's all about, and I don't like it! You've been using me for your own ends right from the start — is that it? And I thought —'

'What did you think?' he asked quietly.

'That — that — that it all meant something more. Instead of that, all you are is some private detective. And what's more, I *am* going straight to the police!' She made a movement away from the car, but Guy shot out a strong hand and gripped her by the arm.

Holding her tightly as she struggled to break away, he glanced apprehensively at the rapidly lightening eastern sky. He must win her over quickly, or it would mean losing what was left of the friendly darkness. 'Look, June, you've put your foot right in the centre of something that may be far bigger than any murder, and I'm trying to find out what it's all about. And by the way,' he added gently, 'I'm not a detective.'

She stopped her frantic efforts to escape. 'Who are you working for?' she flashed.

For perhaps half a second he hesitated; then: 'You, June — and millions more.'

Suddenly all the fight went out of her; she became a dead weight in his grasp. 'Oh!' A long pause; then, very slowly: 'I think I'm beginning to see.' She looked into his eyes; those deceptively lazy eyes she had grown to trust in the long hours of bewildering danger and night. 'And a moment ago I thought you might even be out for your own gain!' She put an impulsive hand on his arm. 'I'm so terribly sorry, Guy, but you're rather a confusing person, you know.'

He sighed with relief. 'Then you'll stay here?' he asked.

She nodded. 'Yes, of course I'll stay.'

'Good. I'll give you the late lamented Mason's gun just in case you need protection, and you can amuse yourself drying out our torch — I'll have to take the good one with me, I'm afraid — but don't show any light if you can help it. I'll be back soon, I hope.' He paused. 'If you'd like to get out of those wet clothes, there's a big leather coat and some rugs in the back of the car, and you'll find a first-aid kit under the front seat as well, so look after yourself. I'll have to move fast now.'

He began to walk away, hesitated, and turned back. June watched him expectantly, her eyes dark and wondering.

'Believe this,' he said. 'I didn't make use of you like you thought. What I'd have done without you, I don't know — you've been wonderful.' Without giving her time to answer, he swung round and made off quickly into the shadows.

Once clear of the hollow, Guy lengthened his stride. He was uncertain what he expected to find at Pardoner's Folly; uncertain for that matter if there would be anything helpful at all in the old house. But it was worth investigation, and his hopes were high as he travelled across the moor.

He hurried on, satisfied in his mind that June would await his return. How much she had guessed from their conversation he could not tell, but it was fairly clear that she now realised he was involved pretty deeply in whatever was going on. It was ironic to think that she knew almost as much about it as he did himself, and yet imagined, he supposed, that his knowledge was far greater. He smiled grimly at the idea. Here he was still groping, though not in quite such a thick darkness as before. Soon, he hoped, he would come out into the light and be able to see everything clearly.

Guy beat the dawn by a short head, creeping silently through the fir plantation surrounding Pardoner's Folly just as the first long fingers of red and gold and flaming crimson began reaching up into the sky from across the sea. His approach had been carefully planned so that he came on the house from a quarter still dark with retreating night, and which was screened as well by the very trees that gave him cover.

At the inner edge of the wood he found himself looking across about thirty yards of rough unkempt grass, high with weeds, which might at one time have been velvet lawn, but through years of neglect had been reduced to a space little better than the waste of open moorland. On the other side of this rose a thick hedge, and behind it again, the southern wing of the rambling house. He scanned the few visible windows for any sign of movement, and seeing none, moved swiftly to the curtain of concealment offered by the ledge.

So far so good, he thought, listening intently. Unless Tyler had already returned, the place would be empty, and he would have it all his own way. However, it was useless relying on that supposition; so, finding a gap in the close-growing bushes, he peered through at what lay beyond. All the windows visible on the ground floor were tightly shuttered, possibly due to the fact that there was very little glass left in any of them; but some yards nearer the back of the building was a French window which looked as if it might yield to treatment more readily.

Warily approaching this entrance, Guy gripped the rusty handle and pushed. With a protesting creak that sounded horribly loud to his keyed-up senses, one half gave an inch or two, then stuck firm. Waiting cautiously for a few seconds, he tried again, putting more force behind his efforts, and this time was rewarded by a sharp snap as something broke and the window swung stiffly inwards. With his gun in one hand and the flash-lamp in the other, Guy stepped across the threshold, leaving his way of escape wide open if it should be needed in a hurry.

The room in which he found himself was large and bare of all furnishing. Black panelled walls threw back the dull reflection of his light; dust clung thickly to everything, so that the once-magnificent parquet floor felt soft as if deeply carpeted beneath his stockinged feet. An utter and complete silence enveloped the place, giving him an odd sensation of being somewhere dead; somewhere lifeless and soulless, almost as if he were invading an age-old tomb. Suddenly feeling cold in the strange substance of uncanny silence, he made for the door opposite, breathing freely again when it opened under the cautious touch of his fingers.

Beyond was a vast stone-flagged hall, the roof lost in a gloomy scaffolding of time-blackened beams; while here, he noted, the dust had been swept from the floor. Casting the beam of his torch round, he made out a pile in one corner, and, tiptoeing over to it, was elated to find a diving suit complete with all its assorted equipment; the heavily weighted boots, the big brass helmet — everything was there.

A good start, he decided. The discovery bore out his earlier guesses in a gratifying manner, and further search might throw even more light on things.

At the end of the great hall, before a wide, empty fireplace, stood a long table, and Guy's eyes caught the white gleam of paper on its broad surface. Quickly crossing the hall, he realised in disgust that it was nothing more interesting than a yellowed newspaper. Purely out of curiosity, he glanced casually at the dateline, and was a little surprised to find that it was no less than six years old.

On the point of turning away to continue a more profitable line of investigation, he noticed something else that made him pause. Black pencil marks underscored a small item at the foot of one column. His interest rising immediately, he bent down to peer at the printed lines, but read no further than the first few words before a tiny sound behind his back sent him whirling round.

He ducked too late to avoid the sudden onslaught of a dark figure. Even as his finger tightened on the trigger of his automatic, his attacker's arm sliced down, the club it held striking him on the temple with a sickening thud.

Soundlessly, Guy crumpled to the chill floor, blind unconsciousness sweeping over him in an icy wave of deadening pressure.

12

A distant roll of drums crept across the endless blue-white glacier. Guy cowered back among frowning icebergs. They soared above his head, threatening to topple forward and crush the life from his body. The drums grew louder, hammering out a deafening roar of sound. He opened his eyes; the icebergs and the glacier vanished in darkness, but the drums played on — inside his brain.

Desperately fighting down successive waves of nausea, he tried to think. Gradually the beating in his skull slowed and stopped. He experimented with his arms and legs, only to find them securely bound. It was pitch dark, and the floor on which he lay felt cold and damp.

Where he was, or how long he had been there, he had no idea. That he was still somewhere inside Pardoner's Folly, he only guessed; and, judging by the darkness and damp atmosphere, it seemed likely that his prison was one of the airless cellars below the old house.

His head ached abominably; his body weighed limp and heavy. Feeling weak as a kitten, he rolled over on one side. For a while he remained quite still, allowing his head to clear and waiting for the constant surges of vertigo to pass.

One thing was apparent: he had landed himself in the nastiest mess he could imagine, for Craig Tyler would hardly let him out alive once he had him in his power. Guy wished now that he had chanced a shot at his enemy before extinguishing the searchlight. But recriminations, he thought bitterly, were not going to be much help at the moment.

The only bright spot in the situation was that eventually, when he failed to return, June would communicate with the police, and through them Sir Randolph would learn how things stood. By then it was obvious that he himself would be past help, but she could give them all the information he could have done — apart from that short headline or whatever it was he had just had time to read before being knocked out. He tried to remember the exact words, sorting out the jumble of memories in his mind and assembling them to make sense. What had it said?

'CAPTAIN RANDALINER, M.N., missing, believed drowned ...' That was all there had been time to read. An obituary notice, of course! He remembered now. It had come almost at the end of a whole column of such announcements.

But where was the connection? The name meant nothing to him, yet the common denominator for all these oddly diverse clues he had picked up was the sea itself, and this one was no exception. 'Capt. Randaliner, M.N.' Merchant Navy. It might fit — must in fact — but at the moment he could not see where. The problem, however, was still interesting.

In spite of his acute discomfort, and the fact that he had already decided his hours must be numbered, Guy continued to wrestle with the mystery. For one thing, it gave him something to do; and for another, although he fully expected to die shortly, he refused to give himself up to despair until the last moment actually arrived.

And so he doggedly turned things over in his mind. Already he had come to the conclusion that salvage work of some sort was the ultimate and only possible aim of Tyler's efforts. Everything pointed in that direction. Suppose then, for argument's sake, that Elgin Crossler, or Tyler, had come to know the position of a foundered vessel? What would be the good of that? Guy asked himself the question and answered it immediately. None, because it certainly would not be possible to raise it in secret, and in any case the *Arrow* would be useless for the job. But suppose again that it was not the vessel they were after, but something she had been carrying! That was much more likely. It explained the delicate depth recorder with which to locate the wreck, and the crane on the *Arrow* with which to haul to the surface whatever it was that had such high value. Probably, too, in view of the equipment he had seen, Pedro was a skilled diver.

And the six-years-dead Capt. Randaliner, M.N.? Where did he come into it? Guy puzzled for a while, and in the end the only thing he could think of was that

Capt. Randaliner might well have been the master of this hypothetical vessel on which was based his reconstruction.

There were gaps, of course — big ones; but somehow he felt sure the bones were there. It seemed a pity that there was little chance now of his being able to clothe them in the flesh of detail. He was glad of one thing, though: if Tyler was engaged in nothing more deadly than pilfering a sunken wreck, however great the profit might be to him personally, Britain would hardly suffer any very severe blow as a result of his activities. It was a relief for Guy to think that if he was to die, he would not be leaving his country with some dire plot against it in the course of being carried out. He felt almost happy. Discounting his own bad luck, things might be far worse. Sir Randolph would quickly hear about it, and June was safely out of it, which was almost as important.

He relaxed a little, wondering what was to happen next; realised, too, that he was incredibly hungry. Time passed with slow deliberation. His limbs ached with cramp, his head was painful in a dull sort of way, and his stomach ached with emptiness.

And then Craig Tyler came to visit him.

The two men had not been face to face since that night four years before in Italy, and it was a strange moment for Guy when into the blackness of the cellar came a shaft of light as an unseen door swung open, to be followed a moment later by the limping figure of his old enemy.

The man set the hurricane lamp he carried on the floor and peered into Guy's face. 'So you are awake,' he said softly. 'It is most pleasant to see you again, Conway — quite unexpected too, I may say, though I'm afraid it will be a short-lived pleasure for both of us.'

Guy smiled. 'You're very sure of yourself, Craig. I remember feeling just the same myself when I threw you over that bridge. What fate have you in mind for me, by the way?'

'You will be found drowned somewhere along the coast,' came the answer; and then, after a pause, Tyler went on: 'I should be interested to know how much you discovered before tripping up.'

'Quite a lot,' replied Guy calmly. 'The reason why you wanted Fortune Cay, for instance, and the purpose to which you intend to put the *Arrow.*' He stopped. Some of it was bluff, but he might yet learn more. 'The only thing I'm uncertain about is what it is that you're so anxious to fish out of the sea.'

Tyler laughed. There was real humour in the sound, but for some reason it made Guy feel uncomfortable.

'My dear fellow, you must have been enjoying yourself! How long have you been on the job?'

'Long enough.' Guy's answer was curt.

Again the other laughed, then: 'Long enough to gain that little knowledge which is such a dangerous thing — and which leads to only half a solution!'

He chuckled, and Guy was conscious of a chilly sensation that had nothing to do with the damp floor on which he lay. 'What do you mean?' He tried to keep his voice steady.

Tyler glanced at his watch, appeared satisfied, and turned his solitary eye on Guy again. 'In roughly six hours, Conway, you

191

will be a dead man,' he began, 'so I fail to see what harm it will do if I tell you some of the things you missed — they'll make you sleep better!'

He paused with a sardonic smile, and Guy reflected somewhat bitterly that now, when it was too late to do anything about it, he might learn all there was to know.

Tyler was speaking again: 'You guessed I wanted the cottage because of its very convenient cave, I suppose?'

Guy nodded. 'Yes, but I'd like to know how you learnt about the secret stairway — after all, Mersey only found out by accident.'

'That was someone else's knowledge, not mine.'

So that was where Crossler fitted, thought Guy. Aloud he said: 'What are you salvaging, Craig?'

Tyler's eyes narrowed, gleaming brightly as it caught the lantern light. 'Wealth beyond your imagination, my friend.'

'In the late Captain Randaliner's vessel, eh?' It was a shot in the dark but it went home. Guy saw the man start slightly.

'You seem to have learned a little more

than I imagined,' he said dangerously.

Guy shrugged — if one can shrug lying trussed up on a floor. 'I don't see that it matters now. You appear to have me where you want me. I'm prepared to accept that — it's just my bad luck — but tell me more and satisfy my curiosity. What are you going to do with all this fabulous wealth when you lay your hands on it?'

'Put a million pounds' worth of gold in my suitcase — metaphorically speaking — and retire.'

'Very nice for you. And how about Elgin Crossler? What does he get?'

Tyler jumped visibly at the name, but recovered quickly with a crooked smile. 'So you know about him, too?'

'Oh yes.' Guy's reply was airy.

'Well, if you really must know, he gets the same share as myself. The rest goes elsewhere.'

It was Guy's turn to jump. 'The *rest*? What …?'

'Several million more.' Tyler was enjoying himself now. 'In fact, quite enough to supply a certain terrorist organisation with sufficient funds to wage almost full-scale war on your European occupation forces.' His words were slow. Deliberately he allowed every syllable to sink in and register its meaning in Guy's mind.

So there *was* more behind it than simply 'pilfering a sunken wreck'. The possibilities were enormous and sinister. Guy knew only too well how hard it was to crush an underground terrorist movement at the best of times. To know that such a movement was soon to be backed by vast resources, and yet be powerless even to warn his people of the danger, made Guy so furious that he let out an oath which brought Tyler's laughter ringing in his ears.

'That gives you something to think about, doesn't it?' It was a mocking question, for the man was savouring his triumph to the full. A wave of despair swept over Guy, but choking down his helpless feeling of frustration, he determined to learn, if he could, the whole set-up.

'And when do you expect to collect these riches?' His voice betrayed none of his inner feelings.

''In a day or two — as soon as my diver gets the exact location.' Tyler paused as if remembering something else. Then: 'Where is that depth recorder, by the way?'

'Smashed!' was Guy's laconic reply. He had difficulty in suppressing the delight he found in giving this news, but to his disappointment Tyler merely shrugged his shoulders.

'I've a second one by me in case of accident, so it doesn't really matter; I just wondered, that's all.' He stood up as the door opened, and a man Guy knew must be Pedro came in. His face crinkled into a malignant grin at the sight of Guy; then, turning to Tyler, he addressed him.

'All ready when you are, Guv'nor; the van's waiting.' His voice had a peculiar accent — like a 'Continental Cockney' thought Guy, inventing the phrase.

'Good.' Tyler picked up the lantern; then to Guy: 'This is where your journey begins, my friend,' he said grimly. 'At low tide this evening, the excellent Pedro will take you out to sea. Until then, we're moving you to the cellar at Fortune Cay in a closed van.'

He chuckled unpleasantly, and Guy's heart sank. There would be little chance of learning anything further with Pedro present, he decided; and, trussed up as he was, no hope of escape from that dread cellar beneath the cottage.

Nor was that all. A fact that puzzled and worried him not a little was the entire absence of any mention of June during the recent conversation. Could it be that Tyler discounted her as not being worth bothering about? Or worse, had she already fallen into the hands of the enemy? He knew Tyler sufficiently well to realise he would never underestimate a risk like that, and the alternative was ugly. Dare he chance a question? He must.

'What happened to the woman?' he asked, afraid of what the answer would be, yet anxious at the same time to hear it. Tyler eyed him coldly. Guy held his breath as he waited.

'Like an imbecile, she came looking for you.' The matter-of-fact words bit into Guy's brain with stunning force. Fate just laughed in his face every time.

'What — what happened?' he ventured.

'Pedro caught her snooping round.' He smiled sourly. 'You'll have the doubtful pleasure of drowning in each other's company.' Then to Pedro: 'All right, carry him out. We've wasted enough time talking.'

Guy felt himself lifted from the floor with an ease that astonished him, hoisted across the broad shoulders of Pedro, and carried up some stone steps to a world of daylight. Judging from the height of the sun and the slant of the shadows, he reckoned it must be some time in the early afternoon. A few moments later Pedro dumped him into the back of a small van, the doors were slammed, and, with Tyler at the wheel, they jotted away from the track towards Fortune Cay.

None of Guy's thoughts were pleasant, nor even remotely cheering. There seemed to be nothing that had gone right. He cursed himself for clinging to his information. The least he could have done would have been to send June on ahead to the police. And now? Now they were both to find a watery grave, taking what they knew with them; information that would have been instrumental in saving hundreds of British lives. He groaned inwardly.

With a last protesting rattle, the van bumped to a standstill, then backed up to the door of the cottage. Shortly afterwards, Guy was being pushed through the trapdoor and into the dark pit beneath the kitchen. His descent of the stairs was rapid and painful, and he landed in a heap at the bottom.

Tyler's voice echoed hollowly down to his ears. 'Enjoy yourself, Conway. We'll be back later.' With a creak, the little square of stone hinged back into place, leaving Guy in a darkness blacker than night.

He tried to shift himself into a more comfortable position. For some minutes he swore quietly but vehemently, sick at heart because of his plight and the pig-headed attitude that had led him into it. And then, with bewildering suddenness, he heard the soft voice of June coming to him from the far corner of the cellar.

'Stop swearing, Guy,' she said very calmly. 'I'm trying to think.'

13

The amazing fact that June was sharing his prison with him took several seconds to register; and then it ceased to be amazing. Tyler had told him plainly enough that she also was a captive, and her presence, therefore, was quite logical. What he could not understand, however, was her wonderful calm and restraint under the circumstances.

'June!' he gasped, vainly trying to see her in the darkness. "Where are you? Why didn't you speak before?'

'I couldn't say anything earlier, Guy, because I was unconscious when they brought me here, and I was afraid they might knock me out again if they heard me speak. I'm all tied up — I suppose you are, too?'

'Like a Christmas turkey, my dear! In fact, we would seem to be in something of a jam.' He purposely kept the tone of his voice light. 'Have you any ideas? I can't move hand or foot myself, and in about four hours from now we'll be pushed quietly off the *Arrow* and left to feed the fishes. Sorry to put it so plainly, but it's no good blinking our eyes to facts.'

'I'm not blinking, Guy.' Her voice was firm, if a little quiet. 'I know all about what's going on. Oh Guy, there must be some way out. Surely it's not going to end like this after — after everything we've been through. It mustn't!' She stopped, and he knew she was fighting back the despair that momentarily threatened to overwhelm her.

'Steady,' he murmured. 'We're not dead yet, my dear. Let's get the position quite straight and see if we can't pull something good out of it. First of all, how are you tied up?'

'Hands behind my back, bound at the wrists. Ankles tied together and then tied again to my arms by some more rope. I'm lying on my side.'

'Can you move your fingers at all?' He tried to keep the eagerness from his voice. Tied up in the way she described, he knew from experience that there was often some slight movement still possible. And if she could use her fingers ...

He waited tensely for her answer. After

a pause of slow seconds it came. A little.' A barely suppressed note of hope crept into her words as she went on: 'Do — do you think I could untie you?'

'It's a chance, June — but don't be too sanguine about it. I'll see if I can get myself over to you.'

Although only a few feet separated them, it was a torturous journey. Bound as he was, Guy found the only method of movement was to lie on his back and push himself along head first by digging at the rock floor with his heels. Slowly and painfully he covered the distance with nothing but her voice to guide him. And when at last he felt himself brush against her, the perspiration was running freely on his body and he was almost exhausted.

'Where's the knot — do you know?' she asked breathlessly.

'At the back, I think,' he answered, turning on his side with an effort. 'Can you feel it?'

For an endless time she fumbled about behind him. His excitement increased as her fingers began pulling and tugging at what could only be the main knot of his bands; and then, with an eager little gasp, she paused.

'It's coming undone, Guy!' she whispered as she set to work again. Never before had such a phrase sounded so sweet to Guy's ears.

'Good job.' He almost laughed at himself. Here was his 'waif of circumstance' proving herself once more to be their salvation, though what was to happen when they were free to move he could not yet decide. There was only one way out of the cellar, and that led down the steps and through the sea cave — surely likely to be a death-trap in broad daylight, for, without a doubt, Pedro would even now be preparing the *Arrow* for its grim voyage that night, and neither Guy nor June was any longer armed.

One thing at a time, he thought; and when presently the cords about his body slackened a little, he was conscious of a wonderful feeling of relief. Whatever lay before them next could be endured or over-come successfully with a much greater ease if they were free to move about. Possibly it was as much a psychological effect as anything else, but Guy found his mind clear of any sense of despair now that he was so near to being released. His spirits rose higher and higher as the cords on his arms grew looser, and when at last he was able to wrench one forearm free, he knew that nothing now was going to stop them.

If they could effect an escape and reach the car, Guy could lay his information before Sir Randolph, so preventing Tyler from gaining his ends. The very fact of their escape would tie the enemy's hands, and that in itself would be a victory.

Once his hand was free it was the work of minutes only before June's were loose. Soon both of them were chaffing and rubbing the cramp from their stiffened limbs and walking up and down the confined space of their cell.

To escape, however, was another and, if anything, more desperate problem to solve. Guy knew the steps leading down to the sea cave were there in the darkness, waiting to be used; inviting them to descend. But he knew as well, though he made no mention of the fact, that below would be Pedro, and possibly Tyler. Unarmed and without even the friendly darkness to help them, what chance would they stand of escaping that way? Yet escape they must! The knowledge Guy now carried inside his brain simply had to be communicated to Sir Randolph somehow or other. Far more than their own lives depended on it, and he felt again that dread that more than once had whispered mockingly in his ear since the previous day. The previous day! Never before had he known so much excitement and danger crammed into the span of a few short hours. 'Fun and games' with a vengeance! And the situation threatened to become even more complex and disturbing. There must be some way out. He couldn't afford to fail now.

He climbed the wooden stair to the trap-door above, feeling round its edges in the faint hope of discovering if it were possible to force it from the inside. The smooth stone fitted flush, however, leaving a barely perceptible crack which was obviously use-less for his purpose. No, he thought wryly, unless they had a tool strong enough to split the stone, that way was out of the question. Whoever contrived the secrets of Fortune Cay in the long-dead past had done his work well, and Guy's thoughts were tinged with a bitter admiration for the nameless craftsman.

Should he take a chance and try the sea cave? If he left June hidden near the bottom of the rock steps and dared a look round in the cavern, something helpful might conceivably come of it.

'Come,' he whispered. 'It's the only way I can think of.' One step at a time, in pitch darkness they crept down, their muscles taut in anticipation, their hearts pounding with tense excitement.

At the first glimmer of twilight that showed itself below, Guy stopped June where she was and went on alone. Crouching in the last shadows provided by the narrow stairway, he looked out into the dim light of the cavern beyond.

Just as he feared would be the case, the shape of the *Arrow* lay a few yards off the little beach, rocked gently by the wave-lets of the incoming tide, while bending down in its cockpit was the figure of Pedro. Apparently he was working on his diving equipment, since Guy made out the dull gleam of the rounded helmet. With rising water, he knew the man must soon be forced to take his boat outside the cave to anchor in the inlet, but until he did so his presence barred any further movement on Guy's part.

Even as he watched, wondering what the chances of a direct attack would be, a faint shout came through the entrance from the outer sunshine, and he realised it could be no one else but Tyler calling to Pedro.

Straightening up, the man cast off the rope which secured the boat; then, reaching down, he pressed the self-starter. Under cover of the softly muffled chug of the engine, Guy decided the possibility of discovery was now slight, and accordingly he beckoned to June in the darkness behind him. To seize the opportunity thus presented and hide in the sea cave while both men were occupied outside was their best course of action; and then, much as he hated the idea, they would have to get out after dark as they had come before — through the submerged entrance.

The *Arrow* swung round and began moving across the water of the basin. June came up at his elbow, pressing close to see what was happening. He put a hand behind his back and touched her arm, keeping his eyes fixed on the boat as it moved slowly towards the cave mouth. And then, with a suddenness that brought a startled gasp to her lips, his warning touch became a steel-like grip. Heedless of noise, and conscious only of a terrible peril, he jumped to the shingle, dragging June with him.

'Down!' he yelled. 'The mine!'

Pushing her flat on her face, he threw himself beside her, an icy sensation crawling over his scalp as the seconds ticked past.

Accustomed to the darkness as his eyes had become after their captivity in the cellar, Guy had seen something which Pedro had missed. Just within the confines of the cave, he caught sight of the dread shape of the mine bobbing sluggishly to the surface as the rising tide gave it buoyancy. *And the* Arrow *could not fail to strike it!*

His shout had reached Pedro's ears as well as June's, and from the corner of his eye he saw the man whirl about to peer behind him at where they lay. Guy pressed his body tight against June's, crushing her to the rough cavern wall, and even as he did so the launch touched the mine.

The whole cave seemed to fill with a roar more fearful than anything he had ever conceived possible. Blinding flame leaped upwards. With a terrific shock, as if he was being struck by some irresistible force, Guy felt himself lifted and flung on top of June. A shower of stones, sand and water cascaded over him. Blinded, battered, suffocated and crushed by the terrible wave of pressure that tore upon him, Guy seemed to float interminably in space; then instantaneously everything ceased, as if a switch had been opened to break the very circuit of life itself.

14

Guy stirred weakly, then opened his eyes. He could see nothing. All about was dark with the darkness of limitless void. Oh God! Not blind, he begged. His mouth felt clogged; breathing was difficult, like sucking fire through his lips. His sightless eyes, too, burned hotly.

Seeming to come from nowhere, a hand suddenly touched his face. It remained still for a moment, then travelled slowly down his arm to the sinewy wrist. Through the constant ringing in his ears, he became conscious of laboured breathing close beside him.

'Guy, say something! Please, my darling, please say something!' The choking words, half-croaked, half-sobbed, broke through from a long way off to reach his brain. Guy felt himself smiling twistedly, barely knowing what he did or the nature of his emotions. *Must be an angel*, he thought stupidly.

'Say that again,' he muttered. 'It sounded awfully sweet.' Speaking the words, he realised it was not the kind of angel he had imagined who was beside him, but his flesh and blood comrade in peril, June.

A faint gasp came to his ears, but she made no attempt to repeat her plea. Instead, she said: 'Are you — are you badly hurt?'

He raised himself to a sitting position before answering. A stabbing pain in his left arm told its own agonising story, and his ankle, too, cried out to be careful. He winced. 'I think my arm and ankle are out of action … and … and, June, I'm terribly scared I'm blinded or something. I can't see a thing.' He groaned inwardly at the full meaning of his affliction, thrusting his hand out in front of him; groping.

'I don't think you're blind, dear. I can't see either, but it's because the explosion brought the roof down and sealed the entrance. There's just no light at all.'

For perhaps a second his heart leapt for pure joy, and then far graver understanding dawned on him. With the cave mouth closed, Pedro blown to smithereens in his boat, and the trapdoor above shut tight, he realised with a prickle of fear that they were completely entombed. Only Tyler had it in his power to release them; and Tyler had been just outside the entrance when the *Arrow* met the mine! Nor would he be likely to let him go even if by some chance he did still live.

Guy felt crushed. He dragged smoky, dust-laden air into his lungs with an obvious effort. He coughed; it was difficult not to. The prospect was far from pretty and could, in fact, hardly be worse.

Better find out some more, he decided, before telling June that they might have to face the horror of a slow and awful death. 'You're not hurt, are you, June?' he asked.

'I seem to be in one piece — a bit knocked about, that's all. Can we get out of here, Guy? I'm a little frightened.'

So she, too, had thought of it, he mused. It was a wonder she wasn't more than a little frightened. His voice was serious when he answered. 'We'd better go upstairs again — there's no hope of getting out down here. Give me a hand, will you — I'll have to lean on you.'

Slowly they climbed the steps. Apart

from his injured ankle — which he thought was no more than a bad wrench — Guy's arm was causing him severe pain, and he knew only too well that it must be fractured.

In the pitch darkness, June gave him all the help she could. Several times they stumbled on the way up through loose stuff that had been shaken from the roof by the blast of the explosion. It was murderous going, and when at last the close walls opened out into the greater space of the cellar, Guy sagged limply to the floor. The small cell seemed just as full of smoke and fumes and acrid dust as the cavern had been, and for a moment cold despair gripped him. Ghastly visions of what their last hours would be like insistently forced themselves before his mind's eye with horrid vividness.

'Oh hell!' he muttered softly, half to himself. His arm throbbed madly. Peril stood close in the darkness, mocking with a soundless laugh, and gloating over the exquisite torture of the slow doom he could see so clearly. Yes, he thought, bitterly, Peril had every right to laugh this time. But it was June who spoke with sudden urgency.

'Guy! Guy, can you feel anything?' She

was on her feet, moving about the littered floor, treading cautiously as if afraid of what might come rushing out of the dread opacity about her. 'Feel anything?'

He was wonderingly puzzled; bewildered by the question. He could hear her stumbling about more quickly, then suddenly she was back at his side again, her breath coming fast behind her words. But it was seconds only before their significance told. He sat up with a jerk that made the pain in his crippled arm bring a cry to his lips. Gritting his teeth, he felt for June.

'Show me where!' Pain and eagerness sharpened his tongue. A draught could mean only one thing in that dread place: either the roof or the trapdoor to the kitchen must have been cracked or opened up somewhere by the concussion from below, and thereon hung a slender chance of forcing their way to freedom. A slender chance indeed on which to lean, but a chance for all that; and before they starved to death in their fearful tomb, Guy was prepared to tear the walls apart with one bare hand if it would do any good.

June drew him into the centre of the floor

and tilted his head back at an angle. Very soft, very faint and very cool though it was, it was real enough — the merest ghost of an air current coming from the corner in which he knew the trapdoor was situated. Could it be possible, he wondered, without pinning much faith on the hope, that when the mine went up, it had jarred the mechanism of the trap and loosened it? What a heaven-sent blessing if it had!

He began to make his way to the wooden stair; but June, anticipating his movement by a few seconds, was already halfway up. He would not, he reflected wryly, be able to do much himself, so perhaps it was just as well she had beaten him to it.

For a while there was silence, broken only by the slight noises made by June as she felt about round the unseen roof. At last: 'I've found it, Guy!' she cried excitedly. 'There's a big crack alongside the trap!'

Guy's heart leapt with hope, but it was short-lived, for he realised they had no tools or anything suitable with which to take advantage of her discovery. How much he would have given at that moment for a humble crowbar or pickaxe! Having neither, he wracked his brains feverishly to think of some substitute.

'Try hammering with a lump of rock,' he told her, but there was little hope of success in his words. She came down the stairway and began groping round on the floor for something large enough to suit her purpose, but after a few minutes gave up the fruitless search.

'It's no use, Guy — there's nothing big enough here.' From despondency she suddenly brightened. 'I'll go down to the cave and fetch a lump from there. Sure to be plenty lying around after the bang.'

'For the love of Mike, be careful,' warned Guy. 'I'm not a lot of good for rescue work just at the moment! Besides ...' He hesitated.

'Besides what?' she cut in quickly.

He grinned in the darkness. This was a fine time to start a romance, he thought. 'Only that you're becoming rather a habit with me, June,' he said softly, 'and I'd hate it if anything happened to separate us ... now.'

'I'll pretend ... I'll pretend I'm made of glass, dear.' Her reply was low, barely audible; and then she was gone.

Guy sat down, propping his back against the wall in a position where he would be able to hear the first sounds of her return. His mind followed many paths during the next long minutes. Chief among his worries was whether or not they would be able to escape. If they failed, it was going to be a slow and nasty end that would stare them in the face from the far extremity of a corridor leading hour by hour through pain and fear to ultimate death. He shivered convulsively in the smothering blackness.

It seemed certain that only by their own efforts would they free themselves, for if Tyler had escaped being killed when the mine went up, it would have been nothing short of a miracle. It looked as if Guy's mission was accomplished all right, though in a way that might have been much more satisfactory. Elgin Crossler still remained, of course; but when Guy failed to return, Sir Randolph would probe deeply to find out why, and Crossler would have little opportunity to carry on with the project in which Tyler had been his ill-fated partner.

Guy would have preferred to have killed Tyler with his own hands and made sure there were no mistakes. As it was, he was not even certain that the man was dead, though the odds were all in favour of it.

He tried to think of ways of passing the time; wondered how long his beloved old Bentley would lie hidden in the bushes before someone found it; devoted much thought to June, somewhere below in the dark bowels of the earth, probably even now groping blindly for something with which to attack the trapdoor. Incongruously, he reminded himself to scold her for coming after him to Pardoner's Folly. That had been unforgivable, especially after she had promised faithfully to remain in the car. It made him furious to think about it, and what made it worse was the fact that he loved the woman, damn it. Yes, he admitted the fact with no reserve whatever, but was well aware that in the circumstances it promised to be a love affair with very little future for development.

Guy swore softly, succinctly, and in several languages. He could see a sticky time ahead, and there seemed precious small hope of relieving it in any way, for on the subject of escaping, his doubts far outweighed the faint hopes that fought against them.

Resolutely, he forced himself into a more optimistic mood, gradually bringing discipline to his thoughts and driving back the fears that tried to undermine his balance and courage. Until every avenue had been explored, he realised it was fatal to give way to despair. Being partly crippled as he was made it hard, but in the end he won his mental battle, composing himself as patiently as he could to await June's return.

How long the eerie stillness remained unbroken, he had no idea, and he was beginning to feel anxious about June's safety when his meditations were rudely interrupted. Totally unprepared for it, he suddenly saw a thin streak of light appear in the stygian gloom, and, almost before he had time to draw breath, the trapdoor above swung down, exposing a square of brightness so dazzling after the blind dark that involuntarily he threw a hand across his eyes to shield them.

An incredulous hope sprang up within him as he staggered upright, but a second later, when he dared to look upwards, it was to see the malignant face of Craig Tyler peering into the cellar. Apparently the man had no torch, or if he had, made no attempt to use it. Instead he merely looked down, seeking to find his captives in the shadows; and Guy saw, too, that glinting in his hand was the blue steel shape of an automatic pistol.

Pressing himself back against the wall, Guy waited breathlessly. The unforeseen development of Tyler's arrival was unpleasant to say the least, for Guy had no illusions that his enemy had come to release them. It was a bitter reflection, too, that now their way lay open, it was still beyond all hope of attainment because of that threatening gun. Fate, he considered, was piling on both the agony and the irony in an unnecessarily blatant manner. As if it was not enough just to leave them there!

He was given no time for further thought however, for at that moment Tyler saw him. The gun swung round, and Guy could see with horrid clarity the small black circle of its muzzle.

'It was good of you to shout down there in the cave, Conway,' began Tyler with a sneering smile. 'I just had time to get out. In a way I owe my life to you.' He thrust his head and shoulders further over the opening before going on: 'Where is that fool of a woman? I should never have let Pedro tie her up — he must have made a bad job of it, or you wouldn't have got loose.'

Guy's brain was racing furiously. He must gain time. The longer this grim conversation lasted, the more chance there was of something happening. Good, bad, or indifferent, it could hardly be worse than their present plight. 'The fact that we did free ourselves saved your life anyway,' he snapped.

'That's as may be, but I will not tolerate mistakes,' came the dispassionate reply. 'I still wish to know where the woman is.'

'She was killed by the explosion,' Guy lied. He kept his voice loud; loud enough to give June warning before she came back and walked straight into trouble. She was taking a long time to find a piece of rock, he thought, wondering what the reason might be.

Tyler laughed unpleasantly. 'So you're all alone, eh? It would be hard to die alone down there, my friend. A horrible death!'

He was taunting Guy. 'And you are injured, too? My sympathy is deep for you. Honestly it is, Conway. So deep, in fact, that I am going to show you mercy in spite of myself.'

He stopped, and Guy could barely suppress the joy that swept over him. He opened his mouth to speak, but before words came to his lips the other continued: 'A mercy I am sure you will appreciate. Rather than leave you entombed alive, I shall leave you dead.'

There was a dangerous silky note in his voice, and Guy wondered how long it would be before that little black circle spat its orange flame and copper-clad lead. More time, just to string life out for a little longer. He must talk. Hold back those searing bullets. Surprisingly, he found his voice cool and steady, almost nonchalant. 'This has rather upset your plans, Craig, hasn't it?' How difficult it was to keep the provocation out of his words.

Tyler seemed to consider, turning the idea over in his mind. At length: 'Temporarily, yes. I have somewhere quite safe to go to in the meantime, however; and later on, when all the fuss arising from the explosion and the unfortunate disappearance of that artist fellow has died down, we shall, of course, begin again.

'I already have the approximate position of the sunken ship, and all that remains is to lift the ingots from the hold. I'm afraid it will mean a certain amount of delay while I equip another launch and find a suitable diver, but that won't take long. After that, my friend, your British soldiers in the big cities of the continent can look for trouble! We are strong now, and growing stronger every day. With such a treasure as will soon be at our command, nothing will be too great to tackle. Your power will be undermined and overthrown in a bloody uprising!' His eyes were blazing fanatically at the picture he conjured up. With a triumphant smile, he went on more quietly: 'But you will know nothing of all that. By then your mouldering corpse will be rotting down there on the cold stone floor!'

'You hope!' Guy was seething inwardly at the man's cool, unruffled attitude. He would not now even be left with the gratifying belief that his efforts had ruined all chance of Tyler and Crossler carrying on with their unholy alliance. In fact, it was, as Tyler pointed out, no more than a temporary setback to their plans that he had achieved. He forced himself to remain calm. 'Tell me some more about this fabulous treasure and how you came across it,' he said.

Tyler smiled. 'Since you show so much curiosity, I will, but I warn you it will do you no good.'

'I'll risk that,' said Guy. 'Go on.' He was gaining time at any rate, though what for it was hard to see. Simply putting off the inevitable end for a few minutes, that was all.

'Early in the war,' began Tyler, 'one of the small countries that Herr Hitler was taking under his protection saw fit to smuggle the whole of their gold reserve to what they considered would be a safer place. My friend Crossler, as you may know, is the owner of a shipping line in England, and by pure chance it was one of his vessels that was secretly chartered for the task. She was only a small coasting steamer, and had the misfortune to be torpedoed by a U-boat on the last night of her voyage.'

He paused for a moment before going on. 'There was only one survivor, and, luckily for us, he was one of our own agents — you met him, by the way. He was the unfortunate Pedro — and somewhat naturally, he kept quiet until he was able to get in touch with Crossler. The rest was simple. Crossler sent for me recently to come over and handle the job of salvage. He'd already spotted Fortune Cay as a likely base, and had also seen Mersey use the trapdoor one day when he thought he was all alone.' He stopped with a grin. 'Does that satisfy you, Conway?'

'Perfectly,' muttered Guy. The recital had sent his spirits lower than ever.

Tyler's face hardened. 'Enough of this!' he rapped, moving his gun slightly. 'I've wasted far too much time on you as it is. Are you ready?'

Guy clenched his fists and sent a tearing spasm of pain shooting through his arm. As he bit his lip to keep back a cry, there came to his ears the smallest scratch of sound from the steps in the floor. June was coming back. There could be only one outcome to that; perhaps a preferable one to slow starvation, he decided. What a situation! He made a frightful decision, condemning her to a quick death instead of a slow one. Sick at heart, he kept his eyes on the man above.

'Just a second, Craig,' he said rather unsteadily. 'We're old enemies, I know, but I'm going to ask you one last favour. Will you extend your queer form of mercy to the woman?'

'The woman!'

'I told you she was dead, but she's not.' He paused, then called softly: 'June. Come up, please.'

Tyler gave a delighted little chuckle. 'All right,' he said. 'I'll grant you that — but don't move!' His warning came as Guy took a painful step towards the downward stairway.

Guy called again, louder this time, trying to see through the gloom as he did so. From the gaping hole in the floor came a queer metallic click he was unable to identify; and then, following hard on it, the report of a gun splashed thundering sound from wall to wall, lighting the darkness for a tiny instant with its livid flame. Guy heard a hoarse cry; a dull thud as Tyler's automatic fell from his fingers; a scrambling behind him; a scuffling above. Looking up, he saw the hole in the roof clear and open. Tyler was no longer visible.

'June!' Guy yelled. 'Jam the trap before it closes!'

Quick as a flash, her lithe figure snaked past him and whipped to the stairway. Even as the slab began to rise into place, Guy saw her thrust the long barrel of a rifle through the narrow gap to hold the stone from its seating.

15

Guy's sharp order, and the alacrity with which June carried it out, undoubtedly saved their lives. He gave no thought as to how this sudden and unexpected miracle had come about. Suffice it to say that the blessed chance of her intervention had halted them on the very brink of the Dark Valley, and that now the way back to freedom lay clear and open before them. Sooner or later, he would learn the details from June, but the pressing need of the moment was to get out of the cellar once and for all before any other misfortune befell them in its grim depths.

Already June had forced the trap further open, hauling it down against the pull of the unseen balance weights, and consolidating her success inch by inch as she moved the rifle barrel further back after every movement. While she worked in this fashion, Guy retrieved the automatic let fall by Tyler.

As soon as there was room for her to

do so, he saw June struggle through the opening and stand erect in the kitchen above. 'Wait,' she called down to him. 'I'll open it fully.' In a moment or two, as she operated the secret device, the trap came down to its full extent. Guy, remembering the rifle only just in time, ducked smartly as it clattered to the ground. Stuffing the pistol into his pocket, he grabbed the rifle and slowly climbed the stairway. As his head came through the opening, June took the gun and helped him up beside her.

They were free! Terror shrank back from the joy in their hearts, and for a few seconds under the spell of glorious daylight both of them forgot past and future danger. Their aches and pains receded into the background, swamped and blotted out by sheer gladness. But all this was only for seconds.

Cold reality soon told Guy that his enemy had fled. A few spots of blood on the dull stone floor confirmed his belief that Tyler was wounded; but Tyler alive always had been dangerous, and always would be. What was more, the man still held the secret to the sunken treasure, and all the time it was in his possession he could pass it on to others.

Elgin Crossler, too, was just as great a potential menace. Somehow or other, both of them must be captured or killed.

The shadows were lengthening into early evening as June ran through to the lounge and pulled aside the curtains. Guy, coming up at her elbow, saw a limping figure hurrying quickly up the track towards Pardoner's Folly, and stifled an oath as he realised the man had slipped through his fingers. He put a hand on June's shoulder.

'Well,' he began ruefully, 'that looks as if it's the end of the party as far as we're concerned.'

She appeared not to be listening, but kept her eyes glued on the track where it disappeared over the brow of the hill. 'Look!' she exclaimed suddenly, pointing.

Guy's gaze followed her arm. In a cloud of brown dust, the shape of Crossler's car swept into view, pulled up with a jerk beside Tyler, and, as he clambered in, bumped round in a wide sweep and vanished the way it had come.

Even had Guy been fit, pursuit was now out of the question, and the only course open to them was to make their way to the Bentley and put his organisation on the trail. He still had the number of the American saloon in his mind, and sooner or later the police would find it. Whether the two men would still be in it, he doubted; but, incapacitated as he was, there was nothing else for it. Somewhat reluctantly, he moved to the door of the cottage.

June stopped him impulsively. 'You can't walk all that way,' she said. 'Let me fetch the car.'

He began to argue, but she was not prepared to listen. Instead, she insisted on putting his arm in an improvised splint, and then brought water from the kitchen with which to bathe his ankle. The pain of both was excruciating, and more than once Guy nearly fainted. When she was done, however, he not only felt better, but saw the force of her argument. She was right, of course; and with their enemies gone, no danger could beset her on the short journey to the car's hiding place.

'I'll rustle up some food while you're gone,' he said. 'It won't be very exciting, I'm afraid, but that can't be helped. I'm ravenous, and I expect you are too. Don't be long, will you?'

'As quickly as I can make it, Guy.' She stopped abruptly, stiffening tensely with an inward realisation. Her eyes shone excitedly as she opened the door. When she spoke again, her words were swift and eager. 'We'll have to hurry!'

Puzzled by the sudden change in her tone, Guy looked at her closely. 'Where does the hurry come in?' he asked. 'All we can do now is lay our information before the right people. If you can drive us as far as the village, where I can use the phone, it'll be quite enough. Admittedly, we both need a doctor and plenty of sleep after all this, but there's no frantic rush.'

She bit her lip. 'But Guy, I think I know where those men have gone. If they mean to leave the country, we may be able to stop them before it's too late! Don't you see there isn't a moment to lose?'

Her words tumbled quickly one upon the other, and their unexpectedness stunned him. Before he could ask more, she had vanished through the door and was hastening away up the track. He called after her to stop, but all he received in reply was a wave of her hand.

For a time Guy watched from the open door, awkwardly conscious of his own weakness, but with all the old excitement tingling once again through his veins. The game was not yet finished. In the mind of the small hurrying figure even now disappearing beyond the dusty hill was knowledge that was going to reshuffle the cards and call a fresh deal. What journey lay before them? he wondered.

Still he gazed across the moor, barely seeing the indigo hills beyond, their marching majesty tipped by the intricate fingers of a rare sunset. Azure and gold, purple and crimson, sea-green and velvet black; all these were blended into a transient, breath-taking picture by that most versatile artist, whose canvas is the heavens; whose pallet the elements.

Guy turned from the door. In his mind was the memory of a small hurrying figure — tattered, bruised, dirty and practically barefoot — yet in spite of all that still eager, vital and infinitely precious. Guy felt suddenly rich and happy. He caught sight of himself in a mirror and grinned at his reflection.

Making his way upstairs to the bedrooms, he rummaged about in search of footwear. His feet were raw and blistered from the fearful punishment to which they had been subjected on the shore and during the climb up the fissure. June's, he knew, must be as bad or worse, and he was elated when presently he unearthed clean socks for both of them. Shoes were a more difficult problem, but here again he was in luck. Mersey's, though a little on the small side, fitted him well enough to pass muster, while in the second bedroom he found a pair of flats that would serve for June.

Feeling that now they would both be much better off, he returned to the kitchen and, with much discomfort and not a little ingenuity, contrived to make a pile of sandwiches and a pot of tea, so that when presently the low rumble of the Bentley's exhaust heralded June's return, everything was in readiness for a speedy departure.

She brought the thermos flask into the cottage when she came. While she filled it and ate a rather stale cake, she relieved the gnawing curiosity from which Guy was suffering. Between mouthfuls, she poured out her story.

'I meant to tell you all this before,' she began, 'but somehow everything went wrong and far too much happened far too quickly. Anyhow, about a couple of hours after you left me and went off to Pardoner's Folly, that big saloon came along from the direction of the main road, and I simply couldn't resist the temptation to try to find out what was going on.' She paused, casting a contrite glance at Guy. He smiled.

'As it happens,' he conceded, 'it was a good thing you did; but go on with the yarn.'

'Well, I walked as far as the rise from which you get the first glimpse of Fortune Cay, and there I came up all standing, because at the fork of the two tracks — the branch to Pardoner's Folly and the straight one that goes on to here — was the car I'd just seen drawn up beside a small van.'

'That must've been while I was still unconscious,' Guy mused. 'I never realised I'd been out all that time. I wonder what the van was doing, then — they used it to carry me in later, you know?'

June finished her cake and helped him to the car before going on: 'I don't know what they were using it for, unless it was for carrying stores or something to the cave. But anyway, there they were, with Tyler and the other man in the car talking together and me about fifty yards away behind some gorse.' She paused as she let in the clutch and turned the Bentley, pointing its nose towards the distant, darkening hills.

'What happened next?' asked Guy. 'And where are we going?'

She answered his second question first. 'To a stretch of the wildest moorland you'll find round these parts. On it stands a house named Platlow Grange — I know my way because we once lived quite near, so just listen to the rest of what I'm telling you and don't interrupt.'

'As you will.' He smiled as the car stormed the first of the switchback hills.

June continued: 'You know how sound sometimes carries an incredible distance? Well, that's how I heard.'

'Heard what?'

'What I'm just going to tell you. Tyler and the other man were talking, as I said, and though I couldn't hear it all — the breeze played tricks — I did hear some of the words, like: 'aeroplane ready' and 'Platlow' — that's the house I mentioned — and 'just in case' and a few more things I can't remember. But it's obvious, isn't it? Tyler told you he had somewhere safe to go to, and if that place is Platlow and they've got an aeroplane there all ready for use — a light one could easily take off from the grounds — isn't it clear that now that the balloon's gone up, and one or both of them will try to fade away?'

Guy considered for a moment. There was truth in what she said, though what they could hope to do when they arrived at the other end he failed to see. Would it be possible to stop them? Somehow he felt very doubtful on that score. True, they were now armed, but he himself was capable of very little real action, and June, after all, was no more than a civilian. Not a very formidable team to put into the field against two desperate men like Tyler and Crossler. However, nothing ventured, nothing gained, he thought, and a look round would do no harm, with always the possibility of good coming out of it. If the birds had not already flown, they might be able to put the plane out of action.

'How far is this Platlow Grange, June?' Guy's arm was paining him, but with so much in the balance he could not afford to let it interfere with their plans.

'About twenty miles,' came the reply.

It was rapidly growing dark, and June drove fast — faster than he would have expected her to under such trying circumstances. It felt odd to be a passenger in his own car. Uncomfortable, too, at first, as her inexperienced hands made mistakes that set his teeth on edge. But he relaxed as they went, for, as she grew accustomed to it, her skill in handling the big motor increased, so that before long it was quite creditable. For the first time in many long hours of danger, Guy sat back and smoked a cigarette in silence, content for the moment to let someone else do the work.

'By the way,' he said suddenly, 'how did you get hold of that rifle? I'd just been kind enough to ask Tyler to shoot you as well, you know!'

She flashed him a reproachful look, then laughed. 'Yes, dear, I know! I was listening most of the time. As to the rifle, I quite literally fell over it in the cave, and decided it would be far more use than a piece of rock for breaking open the trapdoor. Never dreamt I'd have to fire it! It must've been flung out of the boat by the explosion, I suppose. Anyhow, it's lucky for us it was in working order. I was scared stiff it wouldn't fire, or that I'd miss Tyler.' She turned her head and looked into his eyes for an instant. 'I've never wanted to live so much in all my life as I did just then.'

'Or still do,' he added with a smile.

Her eyes were fixed on the road. 'Or still do,' she echoed softly. The gale of wind as the car flew on whipped the quiet words from her lips, but Guy caught them all the same. After that they fell into a somewhat awkward silence, and he contented himself with occasional advice on handling the car as they hurtled up long hills or slowed for sweeping bends. For possibly fifteen miles they travelled in this fashion, June a quick pupil; Guy, in spite of his injuries, a keen instructor. And then both the teaching and the learning came to an abrupt and untimely end.

As June edged round a corner and straightened out, the blazing headlamps picked up the rear of another car in front of them. It was just beginning to move off after being stationary, and Guy saw the tell-tale puffs of smoke as the driver ran through the gears, accelerating away. He saw, too, and recognised, the number plate. Their enemies were there almost within striking distance, and had they been a few seconds earlier they could have staged a hold-up then and there. June, too, must have noticed something familiar about the back of the saloon, for even before he spoke she slowed down uncertainly.

'Isn't that ...?' she began excitedly.

'Yes,' Guy answered, anticipating her question. 'It's our friend's car all right. Stay behind and follow.'

She allowed the Bentley to fall back a little, then settled down on their tail. Fortunately the quarry was as yet ignorant of the pursuers, so that the speed was not high and she had no difficulty in keeping the red tail-lights in view. The road was narrow and winding, climbing up through a shallow valley towards the bare, desolate moorland above. It was not yet full night, but dark enough to give concealment on the shadowed road.

Suddenly Guy saw the white gleam of a signpost ahead, and, as the other car whirled past it, June slammed on her brakes. 'Guy!' she cried excitedly. 'We can cut them off by going up that turning!'

'Go on, then!' he urged. The car lurched forward again, swinging off to the right. He pulled his automatic from his pocket. If they could get sufficiently far ahead, it would be possible to bar the road, hold up the saloon, and, with a bit of luck, effect a capture. His heart beat faster at the prospect. He glanced at June. Her mouth was set in a firm line, her eyes hard as she followed the twisting, climbing lane. An eye for an eye, thought Guy, as he remembered the dying man in the sea cave. So be it; here rode Vengeance, cold and menacing in the heart of a lovely woman. Tonight a murderer was destined to remember that age-old wrath through all eternity.

The bouncing, swaying motion of the speeding car made the pain in his arm acute, but gritting his teeth against it, he hung on to the steel grab rail with all his strength. While Fury drove, nothing should stand in her way.

An unexpected hill sent them dropping away into a valley again; and then, as they turned once more, they caught the distant flash of headlights below and to the left. Seconds later, June stopped the car right across an intersection.

'Here!' she said breathlessly. 'He can't pass now.' She jumped down, grabbing the rifle from the back seat. Faintly on the still air came the distant whine of gears. Guy painfully made his way to her side.

'We don't know whether they're armed or not,' he said quickly. 'I'll wait by the roadside just where they'll have to stop. You cover me from here.'

The ambush was set. The sound of the approaching car grew louder. Guy and June, tense in the gloom of their respective hiding places, waited: Nemesis in the shadow; Vengeance foursquare to the road. Pistol and rifle poised in readiness. These two, intent on dealing justice as it well deserved, stood waiting; Peril ranged beside them with Death on hand if need should be.

16

The whine of gears intensified. Long fingers of golden brilliance reached up the hill as Crossler's headlights pushed away the thickening darkness. Guy eased himself forward, steadying his weight against the stunted bole of a tree. Shadows danced fantastically as the approaching car drew nearer; and then, when the driver saw what lay before him, it came to an abrupt halt almost opposite the place Guy stood waiting. June had dropped out of sight on the far side of the Bentley at the same time as the raking headlamps had exposed its lean shape to the enemy, but Guy knew he could rely on her to back him up with the rifle if it became necessary.

For a moment the two men in the saloon held a brief consultation, and while they were thus engaged Guy leaned forward, thrusting his automatic through the open window beside Crossler, who sat behind the wheel.

'All right, both of you,' he said quietly. 'Keep your hands in front of you and don't make a move, or I'll fire.' Without taking his eyes off them, he raised his voice. 'June,' he called, 'come over here, will you?' Neither of the two men made any attempt at action, but he could not afford to take chances now. Tyler, he noticed, looked pale, probably from loss of blood, but he said nothing; while Crossler, his face pasty in the shadows, was mouthing inarticulately.

'What sort of outrage is this?' he managed to demand at last, trying the age-old bluff of injured innocence and failing miserably.

'This is a hold-up, Crossler!' retorted Guy calmly; and then, as June arrived on the opposite side of the car, he opened the door. 'Get out!' he ordered curtly. As the man obeyed, still protesting, Guy prodded him towards the front of the car.

June, meanwhile, had followed his lead, treating Tyler in the same manner, so that within a few seconds their enemies stood side by side, facing into the glare of the headlights.

Guy leaned back between the lights,

supporting his weight against the radiator of the saloon. 'See if they've got any guns on them, June,' he ordered. 'But keep out of my line of fire in case they try any tricks.'

He waited while she ran her hands over their pockets. Her search produced an automatic from Crossler's pocket. Substituting it for the clumsier rifle, she looked to Guy for further orders. Motioning her to his side, he told her to fetch some cord from the Bentley to bind their captives. As she ran off on her errand, he eyed the men coldly.

'The game is up,' he said shortly. 'You might as well know it now. You've played your last cards. If I had any sense, I'd kill you both where you stand, but the idea of shooting in cold blood never did appeal to me.'

Tyler straightened up defiantly. 'Shoot and be damned to you!' he snarled. But Guy shook his head.

'No, my friend,' he said gently. 'You have the full benefit of a trial for murder with all its slow torture of suspense to face before you die. To deprive you of such a chance to fight your case in public would be most ungallant of me.' He felt weak and groggy, but his words were mocking. This was the end of the trail, and a great wave of ineffable gladness swept over him at the thought.

Crossler, his face working convulsively, tried another form of approach. 'I could make you a very rich man if you should let us escape by accident,' he said. The persuasive tone of his voice with its oily supplication made Guy feel physically sick.

'You're not dealing with your own kind now, Crossler,' he snapped.

He wished June would hurry. His legs were suddenly growing very tired and heavy. The faces of the two men before him seemed to blur and waver uncertainly. He mustn't faint before they were tied up. He tried to get a grip on himself; but at that identical moment, Tyler, noticing his weakness, lunged forward.

Instinctively, Guy tightened his finger on the trigger of his gun. The crash of the shot as he fired echoed strangely up the silent road. There was a scream of pain and the sound of a fall. Guy swayed, and then his opponent was on him like a wildcat. A flying kick sent the smoking weapon spinning from his hand. He felt a smashing impact on his chin and went down heavily to fall on his injured arm. Through a mist of pain and mortification, he heard Tyler slam the door of the car, and a second later came the whir of the self-starter and a harsh grating as the driver engaged his gear. Then the car was sliding backwards down the hill at full speed in reverse.

Guy struggled to his knees as June came running up. Seeing he was alive, she raised her gun to fire at the retreating saloon. Had she been able to do so immediately, she might have stood some chance of scoring a hit; but, unused to the weapon as she was, her action was delayed by the fact that the safety catch was down, so that by the time she had released it with fumbling fingers, the range was hopelessly long.

All this Guy saw, heard and realised in only a very vague fashion; but as June sent two shots crashing towards the fugitive car, he became conscious of the sound of heavy breathing on the ground beside him. Tyler might temporarily have regained his freedom, but at any rate Crossler was their prisoner for keeps.

'Bring the car down here, June,' he

muttered thickly. 'We'll put this one in it and make sure of him.'

When a few moments later she turned the Bentley and drove towards him, he was more fully recovered, and, by the light of the headlamps, was able to make a quick examination of Crossler. His own bullet, fired as Tyler launched his attack, had taken the man in the chest, and he was now unconscious. He would not have very long to live, thought Guy. When, after great difficulty, they managed to bundle him into the back of the car, he told June to drive on down the road in the wake of Tyler.

Long since, their enemy had made a quick turn in an open gateway, and only faintly now could they distinguish the rapidly fading sound of his motor. Guy, however, knew the man must be seriously handicapped by the fact that his right arm was useless; and, relying on that factor, he thought there might still be some chance of overtaking him.

Feeling terribly weak and ill, he could hardly keep his eyes on the road in front, and was relying entirely on June. She was doing wonderfully well. Driving the car at breakneck speed, she took risks on the winding road which, had he been in full possession of his senses, would have turned Guy's hair grey.

Mercifully, however, no accident befell them. There was practically no other traffic about owing to the late hour, and when at last they reached the main road she braked hard and turned to ask him which way to go. Guy had no more idea than she had, but pulled himself together sufficiently to weigh up the various points of choice. He decided Tyler would be unlikely to return to the vicinity of Fortune Cay, and more probably would head south, hoping to shake off pursuit on the busier roads in and around York.

'Go right,' he told her. 'And stop if you see anyone on the road. He can't be more than a few minutes ahead of us, and someone might have seen him go by.'

June had started again by the time he finished speaking, and once more the flying wheels were thundering over the road. The cool night air became alive; in a hurricane of sound, she flung all trace of caution to the winds and set herself the task of making the best possible use of the unleashed power at her command. Guy, beginning to feel slightly stronger now, hunched forward in his seat, his eyes narrowed in an effort to see beyond the beam of the headlights.

It seemed to him hours before they came to a fork, either branch of which their quarry could have taken. June slowed, and Guy was wondering which way to take, when he saw a belated road scout on the point of mounting his motorcycle at the grass verge. Here was luck indeed, he thought.

'Have you seen a big American car go past in the last few minutes?' he yelled to the man.

Startled by the question, the scout hesitated, peering at them wonderingly. 'Something went by a while back going like the hammers of hell,' he replied doubtfully. 'Took the right fork, but I don't know what he thought he was —'

June waited for no more. The remainder of his speech was lost in the roar of the exhaust as she let in the clutch. Just as she changed up, Guy caught a frantic shout from the astonished man. 'Must think we're mad,' he said with a grin, as the road ahead leapt towards them once more. 'Where does this lead, by the way?'

'Up into the hills again,' she said, clenching her teeth as the surface roughened a little and set the wheel jerking in her slim fingers.

'He can't be heading for York, then.'

She shook her head. 'No. If he keeps on this way, he'll end up on the moors above Hemsley.'

'That won't be so good.'

'It won't unless we spot him before he gets there. After Hemsley, there's a network of byroads and lanes all over the place.'

On and on they went, uncertain whether Tyler had turned off or not; uncertain of their destination or the intensions of their enemy. And then, quite suddenly, as they dropped over the brow of a hill, they both saw clearly the double pinpoint of red in the distance.

Swooping down the slope, June urged the car to even greater speed, and the next fleeting glimpse Guy caught of the tail-light ahead revealed it to be much nearer.

For long minutes, the throb of the engine beat waves of echo from the darkened hedges. With a loud smack, the body of a flying bat crashed itself to death against the aeroscreen in front of Guy. He put a hand up and wiped the spattered blood from his face. Fury had the wheel again!

'We're gaining!' June cried.

'Keep it up,' Guy said with a smile. 'You're doing fine.'

The road began to twist and wind again, forcing her to slacken speed. Guy wondered if Tyler realised he was being followed. If he was still ignorant of the fact, it would be of considerable help to June. Good as she was, he had a feeling that once Tyler caught sight of her in his mirror, he would be able to show a clean pair of heels despite his injured arm. Guy was now prepared to back her driving against most things, but Tyler was not only far more experienced, but thoroughly desperate into the bargain.

His fears were soon to be put to the test, however, for after perhaps another mile and a half, June took a corner with screeching tyres and brought into view the rear of the other car not a hundred yards in front. With a cry of triumph she pressed forward, closing the gap until the headlights illuminated the number plate of the American saloon. There was no shadow of doubt that it was Tyler. Tense with excitement, his pain and fatigue forgotten, Guy raised his automatic.

'See if you can pull alongside,' he said. By way of reply, June sounded her horn as if about to pass.

Tyler, unaware of who it was, pulled over to let them through. Not until the long bonnet of the Bentley drew level with him did he realise what was overtaking him, at which point his vehicle shot ahead with a sudden jerk. For a split second Guy saw the man's white face, looked straight into his eyes from across the narrow, swaying gulf, and then, leaning from the car, called on him to stop.

Wheel to wheel, the two motors raced along. Would Tyler pull up, or purposely crash into them? Guy held his breath in awful suspense. For an endless eternity, the hurtling cars seemed to travel bare inches apart. If Guy fired at Tyler, a collision would be inevitable, and at the speed at which they were going, the havoc would be complete.

Tyler obviously had no intention of

stopping. It seemed that he would rather take them to death beside him.

'Drop back a little!' Guy shouted over his shoulder, and June eased her foot off the throttle. Instantly the other car crept ahead, and, as the rear wheel drew level with Guy, he fired three times into the bouncing tyre.

The saloon gave a violent lurch, skidded across the road in front of them, straightened out as the driver regained control, and went on, continuing its mad career. Even from where he was, Guy could hear the hammering of the burst tyre. Any second now it might fly off the rim or jam solid, compelling the man to stop. His enemy was almost within his grasp!

A long corner opened up ahead. The rocking saloon, still travelling fast, was swinging from side to side of the road. A white blur of fencing and the red glint of a danger sign swept towards them. June gave a strangled gasp and braked. In the beam of the headlights, Guy saw strips of rubber flying loose from the rear wheel of the other car. There came to his ears a harsh grating of metal, and the saloon pitched viciously on the bend, then skidded madly into a snaking slide. As if a great hand had thrust it sideways, it vanished through the thin line of palings in a shower of white splintered wood.

17

With a protesting squeal, the Bentley came to a standstill opposite the gaping hole in the fence. Before Guy could stop her, June leapt out, ran to the gap, and peered through. Guy staggered after her, saw her put a hand to her head, and, as he came up beside her, knew the reason. Beyond the fence was nothing but a gaping void. Far below, at the bottom of a sheer-sided valley, ran the silver thread of a twisting river. Somewhere down there lay Tyler, mangled and battered in the wreck of folded metal that had once been a car.

Guy put a hand on the June's shoulder. There seemed to be a sudden finality about everything. The night grew oppressive, and his head began to swim again. He let go of June and passed a hand over his tired eyes. So Tyler was dead, and with him went the secret of the treasure.

'Well,' he said at last, 'that's the end of that. He'll never murder anyone else.'

'I'm glad,' was all June said, but in the shadows her voice sounded oddly strained.

'We'd better go. I don't want to be found lingering round here. The police can be very nosey, and we can't afford that.'

Until then, Guy had been too absorbed to wonder what was to happen next, but clearly their own position needed considering. Could he ask June to drive all the way back to Verity Hall? They could hardly stay where they were; nor, at this time of night, would it be wise for two such ragged and indescribably dirty people to venture into a hotel.

He realised that the only way to avoid attracting attention was to leave the district before the wrecked car was found, or enquiries made about the explosion at Fortune Cay. Eager as he had been earlier to enlist the services of the police, he was now just as anxious to avoid them in any shape or form. On the other hand, Verity Hall offered an ideal refuge, for Sir Randolph could arrange to have the injuries attended to with the minimum of fuss. And, apart from that, Guy was eager for his superior to have a full report of his investigations as soon as possible. It depended entirely on June's strength and endurance.

'How do you feel, dear?' he asked.

'Tired out. Where do we go from here, Guy?'

For a moment he remained silent; then: 'It rests with you, June. I can't drive right now, but it's very important that I reach a place just north of London by morning if it's humanly possible. I know it's a lot to ask, but do you think you could do it? You've been splendid so far, and I'm relying on you. At the other end will be comfort, good food, proper attention for our hurts, and as much sleep as you want. What do you say?'

She sighed, then turned her eyes and gazed at the road. 'But what about ...?' she began suddenly.

'Crossler? Good Lord! I'd forgotten all about him. Maybe he can tell me ...'

Turning abruptly, Guy limped back to the car. Switching on the dash-lamp, he saw the wounded man stir slightly. Guy bent over him. The watery eyes flickered open; bloodless lips moved but no sound came. Was he too late? Too late to learn the secret

258

that would return to some war-torn little nation the millions of its vanished wealth? If only Crossler was not too far gone! Guy had to know that secret.

'You're dying, Crossler,' he said dispassionately. 'Have you anything to say before you go out?' He gave the man some brandy to revive him a little. With a quickening pulse, he heard a rattle in Crossler's throat, but momentarily some vestige of strength seemed to enter the heavy frame.

'What could I say to you?' He spoke slowly, and Guy was hard put to it to catch the words.

'Tell me where Randaliner's vessel sank. It's all I want to know.'

Crossler's' eyes were burning and the rattle grew louder. 'Tyler knew,' he muttered maliciously.

'Tyler's dead.'

'Then find out for yourself.' He gave a horrible gurgle of laughter. Gouts of blood flecked his lips. He choked for a moment, fighting for breath, then suddenly fell back. Elgin Crossler was dead.

Guy turned to meet the wide-eyed stare of June. He felt inexpressibly tired. It was all over. With Crossler died the secret. He was bitterly disappointed at having failed to wrest that knowledge from the dying man.

'Help me get him out,' he said presently. 'He might prove embarrassing luggage to carry round.'

'What are you going to do with him?' June shuddered a little as she spoke.

'Sling him after Tyler.' There was no trace of pity in Guy's voice.

Together they dragged the dead man from the car. After going through his pockets, Guy sent him tumbling over the precipitous edge of the ravine, to disappear from sight.

For a few moments he and June stood gazing down in the darkness. Even as they did so, a tiny spark of fire seemed to grow and spread far below them. Guy made out hungry flames licking through the twisted wreck of the saloon. Slow to start, the fire quickly gained a hold.

'Perhaps it's better that way,' he said as they watched. He turned his eyes on the woman beside him. Her dark hair was touched with reddish light; her face looked tired, pale, and strangely haunted.

Leaning on her arm, he hobbled back to

the Bentley. 'I wish I knew that position,' he murmured as he sank into the seat and June lowered herself behind the wheel. 'The game's only half-finished without it.'

She made no answer, looking blindly into the night, lost in thought. 'I wonder ...' She hesitated.

'What?' he asked quickly. 'What is it?' Pain, weariness, and utter exhaustion made his words sound harsh.

She slipped a hand into her pocket and pulled out the crumpled note Guy had found pinned to the door of Fortune Cay. 'There are some figures scribbled on the back of this.' She passed it over to him. 'I remember noticing them before, but thought nothing of it at the time.'

Eagerly he scanned the tattered sheet, a wonderful hope rising inside him. It was true! Before his eyes were hastily jotted bearings, and a position in degrees of latitude and longitude.

'You've got it, June!' he cried, wild with excitement. 'Tyler slipped up badly there. Probably pulled it out of his pocket by mistake for another piece when he made your brother write this note.'

'More likely it was Pedro's rough calculations,' she said slowly.

'It doesn't matter. The thing is, we've got it! We've won, June! D'you realise that?' Guy was elated. Fate had indeed been kind, but somehow he was faintly surprised at June's lack of enthusiasm. Instead of adding her gladness to his own, she simply leaned back in her seat, peering up at the twinkling stars.

'Will that be the end?' she asked at last.

Had he been mistaken, or had there really been a note of regret in her voice? He felt a little uncertain of himself. Her face was dark and clouded as he looked at it closely, but underneath the lines of grime and fatigue he read something that told him all he wanted to know; something that made his pain and tiredness seem small and unimportant.

With the funeral pyre of Craig Tyler and Elgin Crossler erupting long yellow flames in the valley below, he took her fingers and held them to his lips.

'No, my darling,' he said very gently. 'Life's just beginning. Shall we go to meet it?'

The smile on her lips as she let in the clutch and sent the throbbing car down the winding road gave Guy his answer.

We do hope that you have enjoyed reading this large print book.

Did you know that all of our titles are available for purchase?

We publish a wide range of high quality large print books including:
Romances, Mysteries, Classics
General Fiction
Non Fiction and Westerns

Special interest titles available in large print are:
The Little Oxford Dictionary
Music Book, Song Book
Hymn Book, Service Book

Also available from us courtesy of Oxford University Press:
Young Readers' Dictionary
(large print edition)
Young Readers' Thesaurus
(large print edition)

For further information or a free brochure, please contact us at:
Ulverscroft Large Print Books Ltd.,
The Green, Bradgate Road, Anstey,
Leicester, LE7 7FU, England.
Tel: (00 44) **0116 236 4325**
Fax: (00 44) **0116 234 0205**

THE EMERALD CAT KILLER

Richard A. Lupoff

A valuable cache of stolen comic books originally brought insurance investigator Hobart Lindsey and police officer Marvia Plum together. Their tumultuous relationship endured for seven years, then ended as Plum abandoned her career to return to the arms of an old flame, while Lindsey's duties carried him thousands of miles away. Now, after many years apart, the two are thrown together again by a series of crimes, beginning with the murder of an author of lurid private-eye paperback novels and the theft of his computer, containing his last unpublished book . . .

ANGELS OF DEATH

Edmund Glasby

A private investigator uncovers more than he bargained for when he looks into the apparent suicide of an accountant . . . What secrets are hiding inside the sinister house on the coast of Ireland that Martin O'Connell has inherited from his eccentric uncle . . . ? A hitherto unknown path appears in the remote Appalachians, leading Harvey Peterson deep into the forest — and a fateful encounter . . . And an Indian prince invites an eclectic group of guests to his palace to view his unique menagerie — with unintended consequences . . . Four tales of mystery and murder.